The Mystery at Stormy Point

Seaview Stables Adventures

The Mystery at Stormy Point

TRACEY CORDEROY

SIMON & SCHUSTER

First published in Great Britain in 2019 by Simon & Schuster UK Ltd
A CBS COMPANY

1 3 5 7 9 10 8 6 4 2

Simon & Schuster UK Ltd
1st Floor, 222 Gray's Inn Road
London WC1X 8HB

www.simonandschuster.co.uk
www.simonandschuster.com.au
www.simonandschuster.co.in

Simon & Schuster Australia, Sydney
Simon & Schuster India, New Delhi

A CIP catalogue record for this book
is available from the British Library.

PB ISBN 978-1-4711-7043-0
eBook ISBN 978-1-4711-7044-7

Typeset in Bembo by M Rules
Printed and bound by CPI Group (UK) Ltd, Croydon, CR0 4YY

For Anna, who would totally gallop to the rescue!

Chapter 1

Red's deep brown eyes sparkled and his coat shone in the warm spring sunlight. Since Bryony May had become his owner last summer, the beautiful little bay pony had never looked happier. It was clear that Red adored Bryony, and that she adored him back. In fact, she couldn't have asked for a lovelier pony.

It was a fine Wednesday afternoon in the middle of the Easter holidays. The little seaside town looked ever so pretty as primroses peeped up through the grass and clumps of daffodils dotted the rolling green hills. Bryony had only moved to Brook Dale last summer, a couple of months before her eleventh birthday, and despite a few rocky weeks at first, she had finally settled in really well.

Not only had she become the proud owner of Red, but she'd made some great friends too. She was with four of them and their ponies now, up in a field on the headland, practising hard for 'The 80th Three Coves Gymkhana' which would take place that coming Saturday. They'd been going through their events every day for over a week.

'Good boy, Red!' said Bryony as he finished a series of jumps. 'You didn't knock over a single pole. Well done!'

They had borrowed these poles, along with some barrels, from the local riding school, Seaview Stables. This was where Red now lived and where Bryony had the occasional riding lesson when she'd managed to save up enough pocket money.

Bryony patted Red's neck and he gave a happy nicker. Last week he hadn't been clearing all the jumps. But Red was a very fast learner. This was just as well, because he and Bryony were entered in lots of gymkhana events on Saturday, including a knockout show jumping round called the Chase-me-Charlie. Bryony had always loved jumping, and was very excited about this one. And judging by the spring in Red's step today, he was looking forward to it too.

'I wish Piggy would jump like Red,' Emma sighed. Emma Lawrence was Bryony's best friend, and Piggy was Emma's new pony.

The girls watched as Piggy lazily nuzzled Red's side. Piggy was a plump, sturdy Shetland with masses of long, untidy hair. He was tall for his breed, at around ten hands, and Emma was awfully fond of him, but sometimes she said that Piggy looked – and behaved – more like an overgrown *guinea pig* than a pony! She had got him free from her cousin, Holly, who had recently had a growth spurt and grown out of him. But Emma, who was small for her age, could ride him fine.

'Piggy's improving all the time, Em,' said Bryony. 'And so are you,' she added kindly.

'Do you think we're ready for the gymkhana, though?' asked Emma. 'I don't want to let the team down.'

As Bryony dismounted, she smiled back at Emma. Emma always thought of others! Her pale brown hair was in a neat plait today. She'd even taught herself to braid to look the part. But now Emma looked really worried.

'You won't let *anyone* down,' insisted Bryony. 'Trust me. It's going to be fun!'

The rest of the gang were over by the fence as their ponies drank from the water trough. As soon as they'd finished, Bryony watched as they trotted across.

She felt lucky to have made such great friends. Everyone, except Emma, kept their ponies at Seaview, so Bryony saw them all the time. They'd definitely helped her settle into Brook Dale so well.

First across was Alice on Princess Perla, her beautiful palomino mare. Alice was blonde and very pretty, and she liked Princess to look pretty too. Alice particularly loved to braid Princess's mane. Princess however *hated* being fussed, much preferring muddy hillside climbs or crossing fast-flowing streams any day.

Next came Tornado, a ten-year-old black gelding. Despite his feisty daredevil name, Tornado was spooked by everything. His owner, Finn, was best friends with Bryony's twin brother Josh. They sat together at school and both played in the rugby team, though Finn – unlike Josh – was a real bookworm.

Then there was Harita (Hari) on Daffodil, a dapple grey Welsh Connemara cross. Daffodil was only two and very cheeky. Her new favourite trick was swiping hats off people's heads!

Bryony loved Daffodil's carefree spirit and knew she'd settle as she got older. She did need to learn the ground rules, though, and dark-haired Hari, the decisive one of the group, was firm but fair with her.

The shortest pony pal was Emma's eight-year-old Piggy. He was the shaggiest, the laziest, and quite the *greediest* of the bunch too. If he couldn't snack on lush grass, then he'd nap. And if he couldn't nap, just don't expect him to move!

Emma had only had Piggy for four months, having arrived last Christmas Eve. She couldn't afford many riding lessons at Seaview so Bryony had been teaching her whenever she could.

She'd also helped Emma settle Piggy into his new home: a field and barn up at White Mouse Farm on the steepest hill in Brook Dale. The farm belonged to Farmer Jenkins, a good friend of Emma's dad.

As Bryony stood admiring the little group of ponies, Red whinnied as if to say: 'Hey, and me!' And he gave her arm a gentle nudge.

'Yes, *you're* special too!' Bryony giggled. 'But thanks very much for reminding me.'

With his ticklish left ear, bouncy black kiss-curl and little white star between his eyes, Bryony couldn't imagine loving any other pony more. Red's glossy brown coat was so beautiful too, throwing off rich red tones in the sunlight. That's why, back last summer, she had named him Red.

As Bryony patted Red's neck, she glowed with pride. She couldn't wait to show him off at the gymkhana, and as well as a number of solo events, they were also in some team relays with her friends. These relay events, Bryony knew, were the ones worrying Emma most, because Piggy had to be fast for these – and he wasn't.

One was the 'Barrel Race', where you had to race around barrels in a tricky clover-leaf pattern. When they'd practised it earlier, Piggy had refused to move for six and a half seconds. If he did this on Saturday it would be a disaster! Though Bryony would never say. Emma was so nervous and needed all the encouragement she could get.

Just then the sound of a bicycle bell sent the ponies' ears all of a flutter.

'Picnic-time!' called Bryony's twin brother Josh, screeching to a halt in the grass. Josh was younger than Bryony by seven minutes, and his hair was much neater than her unruly auburn curls. On his back Josh had a rucksack crammed with food.

'I hope you've been working hard for this,' he said. Josh had set himself up as 'Gymkhana Team Coach', but only for Bryony's little group. He might not have a pony but that didn't stop him wanting to be part of the gang, and everyone was very keen to have him around.

'You know us,' Hari grinned back. 'We haven't stopped!'

Everyone tied their pony to the fence and Josh quickly passed round the sandwiches.

'Yay!' chorused the children, tucking in. Working so hard, and the brisk salty breeze, had given everyone such an appetite.

'Oh, blackberry jam – my favourite!' smiled

Bryony. Her mum, who usually made their picnics, had got it spot on today!

As she ate, Bryony gazed across the headland out to sea, which now was a sparkly teal-blue. Puffy clouds, like marshmallows, were drifting through the sky as waves crashed on the rocks below. Framing the cove were neat green hills and behind them was 'town' – if you could call it that. Tiny, cobbled and higgledy-piggledy; the shops were cosy and cave-like and the houses wore the soft sweet colours of ice cream.

Bryony couldn't imagine living anywhere else now. Brook Dale was much prettier than the city they'd moved from. The soft sandy beach with its magical caves was practically on the doorstep. And there were countless fields and flower-filled meadows which were perfect for hacks. No wonder this place was jam-packed with ponies!

The twins lived in Plum Cottage – ancient and magical. It reminded Bryony of the Hansel and Gretel cottage in the old fairy tale with the witch, though sadly Plum Cottage was not made out of sweets!

It did, however, have a wild back garden with a

huddle of plum trees and a swing. After their dad had died last year, Bryony and Josh had moved here with their mum for a fresh start. They'd also come to be closer to their grandpa, who lived in one of the pretty fishermen's cottages.

Bryony brushed a windswept curl from her face and her gaze fell on Seaview Stables to the right.

The field that they were in belonged to the stables and was separated from it by a sturdy fence that skirted right round the perimeter. Red seemed very happy living at Seaview. Each morning before school Bryony would feed and muck him out and after school she'd take him on hacks. In fact she spent so much time at Seaview, Grandpa joked that they should have a stable with *her* name on too!

If you carried on past the stables, for about five minutes on foot, the lane took you further out along the headland, finally stopping at an old disused lighthouse on the very tip of the cliff edge. From where Bryony was now sitting, this old-fashioned lighthouse was partly obscured by a dense bank of trees. She could see the lighthouse's top circular window and a part of the stripy red and white wall just beneath. It always reminded her of the striped sticks of rock you could buy in the kiosks on the prom. Except this lighthouse stick of rock looked terribly faded, as if someone had left it too close to the sunny window.

As Bryony helped herself to one of Mum's home-made pasties, the first butterfly of the year floated by. Now that spring had arrived Bryony was looking forward to being out and about a lot more. And she could hardly believe she was practising for a gymkhana on her very own pony. This was something she had dreamed about for so long . . .

But Bryony wasn't the *only* one thinking about the gymkhana.

'We *have* to win that Golden Horseshoe trophy,' said Hari, crumpling up her empty crisp packet. She flicked her shiny black plait over her shoulder in a very business-like way. Small, powerfully built Hari was a gymnast too. And that meant she was terribly competitive.

'Yes, especially this year,' Alice agreed, 'as the gymkhana's going to be in *our* town.' She brushed a tiny crumb off her spotless hoodie as Bryony felt a planet-sized lump of pasty crust suddenly land in her lap.

She scooped it up quickly before anyone saw. If *only*, thought Bryony, she could be *half* as neat as Alice. Not always. Just now and again. She forced a stray curl behind her left ear but knew she was fighting a losing battle. The brisk Brook Dale breeze encouraged her hair to do as it pleased!

'What are Cockledore and Nettleton like, then?' asked Bryony.

'Well, Cockledore's okay,' Alice replied.

'But Nettleton's very serious,' said Finn.

'We're very serious too,' piped up Josh.

'Yeah, but Nettleton's grumpy with it!' said Hari.

Further along the craggy coast were two more seaside towns like Brook Dale, each tucked into their own very pretty cove too.

Nettleton and Cockledore, along with Brook Dale, took it in turns to host the annual gymkhana. This year it was in Brook Dale, so Peak Point Stables was coming from Nettleton and White Cliff Stables from Cockledore. Seaview Stables provided all of Brook Dale's riders.

But every rider, no matter where they came from, longed for *their* town to win the Golden

Horseshoe, a special trophy awarded to the stable that got the most points overall.

As well as riders from the other towns, Bryony knew she'd also be competing against riders from Seaview. More than anything, though, she wanted to show off Red. He'd been working so hard he deserved to do really well.

As Emma leaned over to pick up a cupcake, Bryony heard her sigh again.

'Don't worry, Em,' she said quietly. 'You and Piggy are doing much better than you think.'

When Bryony had first arrived in Brook Dale, Emma had helped her so much. Now it was time for Bryony to repay Emma's kindness.

Bryony's thoughts flicked back to last summer when she'd been the new girl in town. Then Red had been owned by a girl called Georgina Brook.

Georgina was very stuck up and used to getting her own way. She had despised Red from the moment he'd been given to her as a surprise by her parents, saying that *she* would have chosen a much better pony. Bryony remembered the first moment she'd seen Red in the beech wood. That afternoon he'd been scared of the wind and Bryony had comforted him. Bryony had immediately fallen in love with the little bay, and Georgina had been jealous of the way the pony had trusted Bryony.

Bryony remembered that incredible day when Red had become hers, when Georgina's mother had seen how he loved Bryony and how badly her daughter had been behaving. Emma, who'd been bullied by Georgina too, had finally found the courage to stand up to her at the summer fête last year. But not for herself. Emma had done it for Bryony, and Bryony would always be grateful to Emma for that.

Peeling a banana, Bryony glanced across to Red. She knew Georgina Brook was out for revenge, and the gymkhana would be the perfect opportunity for it.

Georgina had a new palomino now, Beau. Bryony had seen them out in the fields. Pale gold Beau had looked very powerful as they'd practised for the show jumping.

Red, who'd be competing against Beau, was noticeably smaller, coming in at just under twelve hands whereas Beau looked about fourteen.

But Red, Bryony was happy to say, was the perfect size for her. He was also fairly slim around the girth, so Bryony's legs weren't stretched when she rode him and she felt nice and comfortable in the saddle. Although Beau jumped well and was going to be hard to beat, Red, thought Bryony, was definitely in with a shot!

'Hey, Bry,' said Finn, munching on a sausage roll, a huge riding book open on his lap, 'this book I got from the library's *great*!'

'Oh, what are you reading about?' Bryony asked, quickly brushing off thoughts of Georgina.

'Probably everything!' Alice giggled. Finn devoured books.

'Well,' continued Finn enthusiastically, 'the book says it's all about *turns* in the Barrel Race. We need good *angles* it says here.'

'And speed,' added Hari. 'We've got to be *fast* too.'

'Um . . . I've been reading up as well,' chipped in Josh, 'and getting a good start is vital.'

He'd been taking his role as Team Coach very seriously. He'd not missed a single practice session, had brought them picnics every day, had read books on gymkhanas (*three* of them!) and was popping to the stable on his bike to fetch things all the time.

As everyone continued to talk tactics, Bryony felt really excited. She was determined that nothing would spoil this gymkhana, and had every faith in Red to do well.

She picked up a fairy cake and took a big bite. But she'd barely started chewing when she heard the sound of hooves, and . . .

'Look who it is!' said a familiar voice behind her.

Bryony turned and immediately her heart sank.

It was *her.*

Georgina Brook!

Chapter 2

Georgina's white-blonde hair shimmered in the sunshine and she looked as neat and *nasty* as ever.

She was smirking as she sat very upright on Beau, her small upturned nose in the air. On either side of her were two other girls who also rode at Seaview. Eloise was riding Hector, her jet-black Fell gelding, while Camilla was on her blue roan mare called Juno.

Neither of these ponies, Bryony noticed, were as striking as Georgina's palomino. Georgina always had to have the best. Not that Bryony would swap Red for a *thousand* Beaus!

'If it isn't Bryony May and her sorry little . . . *team*,' said Georgina mockingly.

Bryony tried to swallow her big mouthful of cake. She must look like a podgy little hamster! If *only* she hadn't just taken such a Piggy-sized bite.

Georgina's icy aquamarine eyes bore into Bryony's sea-green ones.

'Lost for words?' mocked Georgina. 'About as *useless* as your pony! Thank goodness Mummy and Daddy replaced him with something half-decent.'

Bryony forced down the cake. 'Red isn't useless!' She felt her fists clench tightly. All of last year Georgina had spread this *lie* about Red. Bryony wouldn't have her say it any more!

Georgina now turned to inspect Red, whose ears flicked back nervously as if he'd sensed her cold glare.

'Honestly!' laughed Georgina. 'He's such a flea-bitten nag! My Beau would make mincemeat of, of . . . *him* any day.'

It struck Bryony that Georgina still wouldn't acknowledge that Red actually had a name. Georgina had refused to give him one last summer, joking cruelly then that he should be called 'Nothing' as that was all that he was good for.

'It's time this place,' Georgina announced, now

turning back to glare at Bryony, 'saw that pony for what he is – a loser! And they will soon enough. Only three more days until the gymkhana.'

'Bring it on!' chipped in Josh. 'Red is brilliant, and so is my sister.'

At this Bryony felt her cheeks turn pink. She never felt she deserved compliments, but really appreciated her brother stepping in here.

'We'll see about that!' Georgina smirked, though Bryony thought she now detected the tiniest hint of worry in her voice.

'And my team have got the *relays* in the bag!' announced Georgina, quickly finding her arrogant tone again. She looked Bryony's friends' ponies up and down. 'They hardly look the eventing types,' she said dismissively, as Piggy chomped noisily on grass. 'All *that* one does is *eat* from what I've seen, anyway!'

Bryony jumped to her feet seeing that Emma had gone pale. 'No, he doesn't!' Bryony protested but she certainly wouldn't put it past Georgina to have found out all their ponies' weaknesses to use that knowledge to beat them on Saturday.

'Piggy's coming on leaps and bounds!' cried Bryony, but Georgina simply raised an eyebrow.

Tapping Beau's flanks with her polished boots, Georgina turned her pony around. 'Right, girls,' she said to Camilla and Eloise. 'Let's get back to practice – come on!'

As Bryony watched them canter off she felt all shaky and cross. But that feeling was soon replaced with one of sheer panic.

'Finn – Tor's broken free!' Bryony gasped, catching sight of Tor unattached to the fence, his lead rope dangling down uselessly.

'How . . . ?' began Finn.

'He must have slipped his knot!' Hari cried.

Before anyone could move, Tornado had bolted. Something had spooked him. Maybe Georgina's lot suddenly leaving so fast.

'Tor – stop!' cried Finn. But Tornado galloped off and jumped the fence into the next field.

Bryony and the others raced to the fence and saw Tor disappear through the thick clump of trees leading down to the lighthouse on the cliffs.

'Finn – quick – I'll come with you to get him,' said Bryony.

'And we'll all stay here and mind the ponies,' Hari chipped in.

Bryony and Finn climbed over the fence and hurried off through the trees in the direction they'd seen Tor go. They called his name but the trees were too thick to see anything.

'Try not to worry, Finn,' Bryony said. But last year, when she'd thought Red had been in danger, she'd been terrified.

The waves were getting louder with every step forward. Then Bryony heard another sound.

'Hooves!' she gasped. Finn had heard it too.

'Straight on.'

They sprinted on through the remaining trees and over a big sandy mound. And then in the lighthouse garden they saw him . . .

'Tor!' cried Finn. 'Steady, boy.'

Tornado had stopped just before the cliff edge, thanks to an old picket fence. The fence was very tatty and blown down in places, but thankfully mostly intact on the side nearest the sea.

The black gelding's ears were flicking back and forth and his tail was tucking into his hindquarters.

'It's all right,' said Bryony, edging towards him slowly. Any sudden movements could well make him bolt again, and he could easily break through the flimsy fence. They didn't want him getting *any* closer to the edge.

'Good boy, Tor,' said Bryony in calm measured tones. 'Nice and steady, yes?'

Finn stopped to let Bryony carry on alone. When it came to calming ponies she was the best.

Bryony halted about an arm's length away from Tornado and waited until his breathing was less fitful. Then she started to talk to him again.

'That's the way. See, it's fine. Now how would you like a special treat, eh?'

Tornado blinked. Then one of his ears shot forward. Clearly he was listening and curious. Keeping her movements steady, Bryony slipped her hand inside her hoodie pocket and took out a Polo mint. She always had a small supply as a treat for Red.

She held the mint out and waited. Tornado saw it but didn't step towards her. The hairs around his bottom lip bristled.

Bryony knew from experience not to push things too fast. She held her ground, talking gently, the sweet still in her outstretched hand. Eventually

Tornado gave a small relaxed snort, then leaned in and snaffled up the Polo.

'There,' said Bryony. 'Red won't mind sharing his mints with *you*.'

While the pony was distracted, enjoying his treat, Bryony gently took his reins.

'Come on then,' she said, giving a gentle pull, and he obediently followed her into the middle of the lighthouse garden where Finn was still waiting.

'Thanks, Bry,' Finn said gratefully as she passed him the reins.

'No problem,' smiled Bryony. 'See, he's fine.'

As Finn turned to lead Tor back to the others, Bryony saw him stop and point up to the lighthouse.

'What's that?'

'Where?' said Bryony, looking up too.

'There,' replied Finn. 'Through the cottage window, see . . . ?'

Attached to the lighthouse was an old stone cottage where the lighthouse keeper must have lived long ago.

Both the lighthouse and the cottage had seen better days. The window frames had curls of peeling paint and one window was completely boarded up. Tiles were also missing from its roof, leaving gappy black holes, like fallen-out teeth. This place, everyone knew, had been empty for years. Though Bryony had to agree with Finn, it certainly wasn't empty right now . . .

The window to the right of the front door glowed, as if a candle had been lit inside. Thick cobwebs clung to the panes of glass, making seeing in rather foggy. Nevertheless, Bryony could make out a dark grey blurry shadow moving around inside.

'Ah, right . . .' Finn's voice was a whisper now. 'Last night the stars were, well . . . *odd*, so I checked in one of my space encyclopaedias, and their appearance pointed to a significant shift in ectoplasm that would facilitate paranormal activity.'

'You what?' whispered Bryony.

'*Ghosts*,' replied Finn. 'Popping out everywhere. The stars pointed to it last night.'

'Oh, right!' Bryony nodded. 'But, actually . . . no . . . I don't think so.'

She explained that animals were a very good judge of when things were weirdly odd.

'And look!' Bryony pointed at Tornado, now calm.

'If *he's* not spooked, Finn,' Bryony said, 'then there *are* no spooks in there, I'd say. Besides, ghosts don't make *shadows*, do they? Only solid bodies do that. Ghosts are all shimmery and see-through, you know?'

'Hmmm, you might have a point,' muttered Finn. 'So what's making the shadow, then, Miss Swann?'

Ebony Swann was a quirky tightrope-walking detective on Bryony's favourite TV show. Bryony's friends said she was like Ebony all the time, which Bryony actually rather liked. Why not, when Ebony never failed to solve a mystery and could tightrope-walk across crocodile-filled swamps? Bryony often daydreamed about being a *pony-riding* Miss Swann. And just like Ebony, she had always loved a good mystery to solve.

Brook Dale, however, was quite low on mysteries. Unless you counted helping the postman track down parcels he'd accidentally left on random walls. Or figuring out why the fish shop had shut a whole five minutes early last Thursday for no apparent reason. At least, thought Bryony, 'The

Stormy Point Lighthouse Mystery' finally looked like a meaty one!

Her gaze left the lighthouse and she looked back at Finn. 'So, it's more like *who's* making the shadow,' she said. Bryony knew she wouldn't rest until she found out more. But that would have to wait. There was still daylight left. Time for more practice. If they didn't master those Barrel Race moves Georgina's team really *would* wipe the floor with them on Saturday.

'Right, Finn!' said Bryony. 'Time to get back to the others. Come on.'

Chapter 3

The last hour of practice went well and all the ponies were focused. Piggy even *moved* when he was asked to (mostly).

Alice had a great dressage run-through and Bryony managed another clear round of jumps. The Chase-me-Charlie show jumping on Saturday had the reputation of being very competitive. Once your pony refused a fence, or knocked one over, you were out.

They decided to end the day with a Pole Bending run-through. As Hari set out the poles, Bryony held Daffodil, who nuzzled Red's side playfully.

'I saw that, Miss Daffodil,' Hari called firmly. 'It isn't playtime just yet!'

'She looks so guilty,' Bryony giggled as Daffodil's tufty little ears flopped down.

'I should think so too,' Hari replied. 'This gymkhana won't win itself on Saturday, you know!'

When the poles were at regular intervals, the ponies wove in and out of them in the order they'd go on the day. Josh was timing them with his stopwatch and as the last rider crossed the finish line he punched the air with a smile.

'That was your best ever time', he announced.

'Hooray!' everyone cheered. What a perfect way to end the practice!

It was starting to get dark, and Bryony offered to ride with Emma up the hill to Farmer Jenkins's barn.

'Thanks, Bry,' replied Emma, looking very grateful.

'No worries,' Bryony smiled.

They said goodbye to the others all heading back to Seaview, arranging to meet again tomorrow at two. As they rode away Bryony hoped that Emma didn't feel too different because Piggy was the only pony not living at Seaview. Emma's parents were divorced and she and her little brother, Will, lived with their dad, who was head gardener at Georgina's posh house, Brook Dale Manor. This was where the gymkhana would be held, and Bryony knew that the gardens and fields would look beautiful, all thanks to Emma's dad. She also suspected the Brooks didn't pay him that much because Emma's house, Gardener's Cottage, came with the job. So in return for Emma's dad helping the farmer with his lambing, Jasper Jenkins was letting Piggy borrow one of his fields and barn.

The ponies headed up the steepest hill in the cove, even higher than the cliffs overlooking the sea.

'Why's it called White *Mouse* Farm,' asked Bryony, 'when Farmer Jenkins has *sheep*?'

'Oh, there's an old myth,' replied Emma, 'that the Pied Piper took all the rats (and some mice!) into that hill in the fairy tale.'

'Ah, right!' Bryony giggled. This ancient seaside town was full of curious myths and legends.

Bryony was really happy to keep Emma company on the steep and bumpy way back. Since she'd first come to Brook Dale last summer Bryony had seen Emma almost every day. At first she'd missed her city friends, Becky and Fran, worrying she'd never find such good friends again. But then she'd met Emma, who was kind and thoughtful, and already they'd been through so much together. Now Bryony had no doubt that wherever they were, she and Emma would be best friends for ever!

On their way up, the girls passed a few small farms. Emma kept her eyes firmly on the path, though Bryony glanced out to sea where the sun was setting on the horizon. Its amber glow was casting big orange stripes across the water, like a great sleepy tiger stretched out and having a nap.

Down below them, and jutting out into the sea, she also spied the old lighthouse again, the sea swirling and crashing against the rocky headland on which it was perched.

Suddenly Bryony remembered the mystery shadow.

'Em,' she said. 'Um, this afternoon me and Finn saw something – or some*one* – inside the Stormy Point Lighthouse.'

'What? No, you can't have. Not in there,' replied Emma. 'That place has been locked up for years.'

'Do you know anything about it?' Bryony asked, keen to find out more.

'Only that there was some sort of tragedy,' said Emma. 'And nobody's lived there since. I think it happened a long time ago.'

Bryony thought for a moment as they continued uphill. 'Well, I *definitely* saw a shadow in there,' she said.

'A shadow?' repeated Emma. She sounded a little nervous.

'Of a person,' continued Bryony. 'Finn thought it was a ghost but—'

'A g-ghost?!' gulped Emma so suddenly that Piggy snorted in surprise. 'I'm *really* glad you offered to walk me back now. That's so spooky, Bry.'

'But interesting too, don't you think?' said Bryony. 'There's definitely something going on in there.'

'Can we just maybe talk about happy things instead?' asked Emma.

Bryony could see that Emma was nervous so let the subject drop. But mysteries to Bryony were like itches that needed to be scratched!

The hill was getting steeper and steeper as they

went. Judging by the spring in Red's step, he wasn't tired and was enjoying the hack, but Piggy was altogether more dawdle-y. Finally they stopped at a tin sign swinging from a rusty shepherd's crook. The sign was in the shape of a sheep with faded letters upon it that said:

'Home, Piggy!' smiled Emma, as Bryony dismounted and opened a big iron gate. Beyond this gate was a path through the daisies leading to a rambling stone farmhouse.

Bryony looked around. It felt like she was standing at the very top of the world! The sheep dotted about were like cotton wool balls, all fuzzy and soft and white. And the lambs were so bouncy it looked like they had springs on their feet!

Various farm cats, and recently a new host of kittens, had kept Piggy company every day since he'd arrived. The girls were greeted by two of these cats now – sitting, like stone statues, on the drystone wall either side of the gate. One was a solid stripy tabby and the other a much scruffier ginger tom. These were the parents of the kittens that had mewed their way into the world a few weeks ago.

'Hello, Daisy,' Bryony said to the mum.

'And, hello, Gingersnap!' Emma said to the dad.

Both cats closed their eyes and purred as Bryony led Red in through the gate and Emma followed behind on Piggy.

The girls continued past the old stone farmhouse and into the field with Piggy's barn. Bryony liked this field very much. Now it was sprinkled with primroses but it would have pale purple clover in the summer. There were plenty of trees for shade or shelter too, and the large barn where Piggy had slept since winter had been done up by Emma's dad and Farmer Jenkins to make a very cosy stable.

They took Piggy inside. There was room for Red too and there were countless kittens *everywhere* – chasing each other and tumbling over the hay bales!

Most of them carried on playing regardless, but a few watched as Emma dismounted and Bryony tied Red to a post. Then Emma got on with brushing Piggy down before she settled him for the night.

As she did that, Bryony showed Red the cutest of the kittens. It was a tiny ginger boy, the runt of the litter, that all the others seemed to pick on or ignore. Red's ears flew forward and he leaned in closer.

'Pretty, eh, Red?' Bryony said and Red let out a sharp little whinny.

'Now, now, Red,' grinned Bryony. She knew that tone. 'It doesn't mean I like him more than you. I'll always love you best, you know that!'

When Emma had finished settling Piggy, Bryony rode Red back to Seaview and Emma walked with them. Bryony made sure that this time around she only talked about happy things, planning lots of sleepovers after the gymkhana and before school started.

The girls parted at the stables. Emma went home

and Bryony went in to see to Red. As she gave him his nightly brush down and treated him to a supper of hay, she found herself wondering about the Stormy Point Lighthouse again. Was the shadow still inside? And who actually was it? And what if, when she went outside in a minute, the light at the top that had been dim for years was actually *shining* again? Just the thought of that sent a tingle up her spine, especially as the stables were practically deserted. Usually it was a hive of activity, but not often at this time of day.

When Red's straw was raked about, just how he liked it, Bryony gave him a goodnight hug.

'Night, night, then!' she said, and he snorted back softly, his ears floppy.

Outside on the lane, stars were filling the sky, twinkling like little fireflies. Bryony stopped for a moment and watched them, thinking. Then suddenly gripped with a daring impulse, she hurried down the gently sloping lane to the sea, leaving the stables up behind her – first past their practice field on the left, then the dense patch of trees Tor had bolted through. To the right was the hill leading up to White Mouse Farm, where the sheep high above now looked like grey rainclouds, the last embers of daylight fading fast.

The lane flattened out. Then Bryony stopped as the lighthouse garden came into view. And there it was! On the edge of the cliff, towering up into the sky as waves crashed on the rocks far below: the tall, black silhouette of the Stormy Point Lighthouse.

Bryony held her breath, watching its topmost window, half willing the light to suddenly flicker on, and half terrified that it might. The breeze blew her hair. An owl swooped through the night. Then she turned and ran all the way home!

Chapter 4

Next morning, Bryony stopped to grab a quick bite of toast on her way out to meet Emma and Piggy. Her mum was up early having breakfast too.

'More practice today?' Mum said with a smile.

'This afternoon,' Bryony nodded. 'The ponies need a bit of a rest this morning so me and Emma are just off for a gentle hack. Then we'll meet up with the others after lunch.'

'Ah,' said Mum, sipping her coffee. 'I see.'

Bryony was glad to see Mum looking so happy. She was working as a florist again, from home, and this weekend she was doing the flowers for a big local wedding.

Bryony ate her toast in the window seat, the

sun warming the back of her neck. She loved everything about this kitchen – the dark-blue Aga, the deep cosy alcoves and the thick lopsided walls. She especially loved the cool worn-smooth stone floor.

She swallowed her toast, gulped down her apple juice, then gathered her riding things. After the gymkhana there was another whole blissful week of holiday freedom stretching out. More hacks! Or she could explore new places – or have more fun picnics with her friends. She'd also promised Grandpa she'd help him out with a bit of planting at the allotment. Perhaps Josh, Emma and Finn would come along too!

'See you later, Mum,' she called from the door, and Mum looked up from her newspaper and waved.

'Enjoy your ride!'

Bryony hurried out and down the lane, past the three cows in the opposite field who always watched her come and go over the wall. 'Morning, Nutmeg, Teasel and Bluebell!' she giggled. Those weren't their real names. She'd made them up as she didn't have a clue what they were really called.

Life was like that around here. You just made it up as you went along half the time!

At the stables, Bryony fed Red and mucked him out, then met Emma and Piggy on the lane.

'Hi, Em, coming to the beach?' Bryony asked as Red gave Piggy a morning nuzzle.

'Sure,' smiled Emma, and they set off down the lane.

The beach was nice and quiet as it was still quite early. 'I hope it stays this sunny for the gymkhana,' said Bryony as they rode their ponies along the sand. The waves were small and frilly, and gulls fluttered through the sky like kites.

'Dad's checked the forecast and he said it would be fine,' replied Emma.

Bryony gave Red's flanks a little kick and he broke into a gentle trot. A whisper of a breeze rippled through his shiny black mane.

With a grunty snort Piggy started trotting too, but he always struggled to keep up with Red's longer strides. Bryony glanced behind. Piggy was all over the place and Emma was holding on for grim life.

'Relax the reins, Em, just a bit,' Bryony called.

'After Saturday we can go on lots more hacks to smooth out the trotting.'

'Okay!' Emma squeaked.

'You're doing really well,' called back Bryony.

They trotted on to the end of the beach and Bryony's eyes searched out the lighthouse up on the clifftop again. Since seeing that shadowy figure in the window, the familiar landmark had suddenly taken on an air of captivating mystery. It seemed now to be constantly pulling her towards it, like a magnet.

'Hey, Em – let's ride out to the lighthouse!' said Bryony.

'Aw, I hoped you'd forget about that,' replied Emma.

'As if!' laughed Bryony. 'You know me. Anyway, it'll be fine. How could there be *ghosts* on such a beautiful day?'

She started to head off.

'No – wait!' called Emma. 'I asked Dad more about the lighthouse last night and he said someone died there, years ago – saving a fishing boat in a terrible storm.'

'Oh no!' gasped Bryony. 'Somebody died? Who? Was it the lighthouse keeper?'

'I'm not sure,' answered Emma. 'But whoever it was, what if their ghost has come back? Or never *left* or something?'

Bryony thought for a moment. 'It's not like I'm going inside though, is it? I only want another *tiny* peep, that's all.'

They rode up the sandy path off the beach which brought them out on Lighthouse Lane by Seaview. The stables looked much busier than usual as children bustled about polishing saddles or oiling hooves in preparation for the gymkhana. Right after their lighthouse adventure and lunch it was straight back to practice, thought Bryony!

They rode past the stables, then downhill past the practice field, and then the mini-forest of dense trees. When the slope flattened out and they neared the lighthouse, even though Red felt very relaxed, Bryony could suddenly feel butterflies in her tummy as she buzzed with nervous excitement.

'I'm not sure about this, Bry.' Emma frowned.

'Don't worry,' replied Bryony. 'I promise we won't stay long.'

Bryony dismounted in the lighthouse garden, and walking Red through the sea lavender leaves, she stopped at the old picket fence. When she'd checked to make sure it was secure, she carefully tied Red to it.

'Em, will you stay here with Red while I take a look through the window?'

Emma nodded back.

'But, Bry – be careful.'

'I will,' whispered Bryony, wondering why she was suddenly whispering.

As Bryony was about to set off through the garden, she noticed Piggy looking at something over her shoulder. Emma, who was about to dismount, had noticed him too.

Bryony turned. Was it something in the lighthouse window? But no – Piggy went shooting past her after a tasty-looking patch of grass.

'*Piggy!*' shrieked Emma, forgetting all she'd been taught and lolloping about in the saddle. But Piggy was on a mission! And as he dived for the grass, Emma went sliding right over his neck and landed sprawled in a clump of sea lavender leaves.

'Em! Are you okay?' Bryony rushed over as Emma scrambled to her knees. But Emma seemed more concerned about her pony.

'Stop, Piggy!' shrieked Emma. 'Bry – behind you – *the door*!'

As Bryony turned she heard a low deep *creeeakkkk* as the lighthouse door started to open. They were about to find out if Finn was right, because whatever was *in* the lighthouse cottage was now clearly heading *out* of it . . .

*

Bryony shut her eyes. She was imagining all sorts. Who was coming out? A pirate, complete with parrot and wooden leg? Or a modern-day smuggler maybe? Or *could* it be the ghost of that old lighthouse keeper?!

She could hear Red snorting, and Emma groaning, and Piggy munching grass. Her heart was in her mouth as she half-opened one eye . . .

'Oh!'

There on the doorstep stood a normal old lady. No parrot, no treasure chest, no clanking chains. Just a short, stout old lady with thick white hair cut into a neat bob. She was wearing a blue tweed skirt and a mustard-coloured jumper, and had a pale lilac scarf with white dots round her neck.

How had she got into the lighthouse? wondered Bryony. The place showed no sign of having been broken into. The only other way in, she assumed, was by using the proper key.

The old lady, Bryony also deduced, wasn't a resident of Brook Dale. Everyone knew everyone in this little town, and Bryony had never seen her before.

So where was she from? And what did she want with the lighthouse to visit it two days in a row? As she wasn't a ghost (and looked friendly enough), Bryony decided to simply ask her. After all – if you don't ask, you don't get, Ebony Swann said all the time. And Bryony was determined not to let this *proper* mystery pass.

Bryony opened her mouth but the old lady spoke first.

'Are you all right, dear?' she called to Emma, who was still knee-deep in sea lavender.

Emma, who looked like she *had* just seen a ghost, managed a vacant-looking nod. 'I-I'm fine.'

'Ah, that's good,' the old lady replied, nodding back.

'I'm sorry we disturbed—' Bryony began. But what exactly *had* they disturbed her doing?

'Um, I hope you don't mind me asking,' continued Bryony, 'but why do you keep coming to the lighthouse? We saw your shadow yesterday too.'

'Ah, yes – I'll explain,' the old lady smiled. 'But first . . .'

She walked over to Piggy, took his reins and, when Emma had got up, passed them to her.

'I saw through the window he's yours,' she said. 'I'm Lavender Jones, by the way.'

'Oh, thanks.' Emma blushed as Piggy had been so naughty. 'I'm Emma.'

'And I'm Bryony,' said Bryony.

The old lady looked at her and Bryony now saw that her eyes were a lovely shade of blue and she had a kind, clever-looking face.

She reminded Bryony a bit of her granny, the one who'd been married to Grandpa Wallace for almost fifty years before she'd died. Bryony's Granny Matilda had been very sweet and had made the best trifles Bryony had ever tasted.

'Well,' said Emma, 'we'd better be off.' But Bryony was desperate to stay a little longer and piece together the mystery a bit more!

Just then she noticed the patch of sea lavender leaves (that Emma had just well and truly flattened!).

'Wait, you're *Lavender . . .*' said Bryony, glancing back to the old lady. 'As in . . . *sea lavender*?' she asked.

The old lady nodded. 'Yes, dear – exactly that!'

Bryony noticed that Lavender had a foreign-sounding accent. One of Bryony's teachers in the city had had an accent a bit like it. That teacher was called Mrs Stewart and had come from Australia.

'You're thinking I sound different,' Lavender said. 'You're wondering where I was born?'

'I-I didn't—' began Bryony. But she stopped. The old lady was, in fact, quite right!

Bryony *was* very curious to find out everything about her now. And it seemed she wasn't the only one . . .

From over by the fence, Red let out a loud nicker as if to say, 'Excuse me but *I'm* here too!'

The old lady looked over and her eyes lit up as she saw him properly for the first time.

'Oh, what a dear little fellow!' she gasped. 'I once had a friend who had a bay too, with a lovely glossy coat, just like yours.'

'He's called Red,' beamed Bryony, always thrilled when someone paid him a compliment.

They wandered over and Bryony watched as Lavender gently stroked Red's face. He seemed completely relaxed, standing still and calm. He even let her tickle him behind the ears.

'Wow!' gasped Bryony. 'He must really like you. Red's usually very picky about who he lets tickle him!'

'He's adorable,' beamed Lavender, completely entranced. 'And he smells of . . . oh, cinnamon whirls!'

'I know!' nodded Bryony. 'I smell it too! But not everyone can,' she added. 'Back in the city where I used to live there was this amazing cake shop. Clara's, it was called! I used to go there every Saturday after riding with my dad. And Red's smell reminds me of really happy afternoons.'

'I love cakes,' said Lavender. 'And baking too. And I especially like making lavender cake as the smell always transports me back home to a little lighthouse on the cliff.'

Bryony thought for a moment, then meeting Lavender's eyes . . .

'*This* little lighthouse on a cliff?' asked Bryony.

Lavender, she thought, looked so settled here. Just like she belonged.

'Hmmm . . .' Lavender nodded, a misty look in her eyes as if remembering a happy time long ago. Then, blinking, she smiled. 'Good detective work, dear! Yes, I used to live in this very lighthouse, with Mother and Father and our dear ginger cat, Marmalade.'

'So your father was the lighthouse keeper?' Bryony blurted. 'Oh – sorry, I shouldn't be so nosy!' She felt really bad for bringing that up when he *might* have been the one that died.

'No, don't worry,' Lavender replied. 'I am nosy too! When we lived here it wasn't a working lighthouse. But even so Father did look out for boats. It was just in his nature to help – and care, I think.'

Emma gently nudged Bryony's arm. 'We'd better get going, Bry,' she whispered but Bryony was deep in thought.

'Um, Lavender,' said Bryony. 'Why . . .'

'. . . am I here?' Lavender finished Bryony's question for her and Bryony nodded back.

'Well,' said Lavender, looking back at the

lighthouse. 'I'm here to say hello again. And then goodbye. For ever.'

Lavender tried to hide the look of sadness now seeping across her face. But they didn't call Bryony Ebony Swann for nothing – she'd *seen* it.

She had so much more she wanted to ask. Like, why had Lavender left here all those years ago? And who had she left with? And *was* her dad the person who'd died saving that fishing boat long ago? And why had she chosen *now* to come back to say goodbye for ever . . . ?

Just then Red nudged Bryony's arm too.

'All right. Time to go,' Bryony grinned. She had to get Red back to Seaview as he was giving someone a riding lesson at midday.

Last summer, Grandpa had helped buy Red by selling his old vintage car. But they didn't have enough money to stable him at Seaview on a full livery basis. This meant that Bryony had to muck Red out and exercise him every day. He also had to give others the odd riding lesson. But Bryony didn't mind. Not after last year when, thanks to Georgina, she'd almost lost Red for ever.

'Um, Lavender,' said Bryony. 'When do

you leave? I hope we'll meet again before you go?'

Lavender smiled. 'I leave at lunchtime on Monday. I'm staying in The Ticklish Trout until then, so do call by if you've time. It would be lovely to see a familiar face.'

'Oh, I know that B&B!' Emma nodded. Bryony did too. It was a really funny name for a B&B but it was meant to be quite nice.

'Bye then,' said Bryony, swinging up into the saddle and Lavender waved back.

'Bye,' she smiled. 'Oh! And safe riding.'

As the girls trotted off, Bryony imagined Finn's face when she told him who the 'lighthouse ghost' was! She also hoped Lavender would tell them more of her story before she left for good.

A story, felt Bryony, that wasn't *over* quite yet . . .

Chapter 5

When the girls had dropped off their ponies they went to Bryony's for lunch. After their eventful morning, they'd worked up quite an appetite.

'Oh, I'm so sorry, girls!' cried Bryony's mum, as they headed in through the back door. The kitchen looked like a flower shop – there were hundreds of roses everywhere! Vases on the thick stone window ledge, jugs on the big kitchen table. And Blueberry Muffin, Bryony's grumpy grey cat, was battling a curling tendril of ivy in one of the hand-tied posies in a vase on the window seat.

'I completely lost track of time!' said Mum. 'Lunch! I'll do that now. Right, what do we have?'

She jumped up from the long kitchen bench and hurried across to the fridge.

'It's okay, Mum,' Bryony smiled. 'We've got plenty of time. We're not meeting the others until two.'

'Oh, good! Well, how about a pasty and some toast?' Mum looked a little less flustered.

'That sounds great,' said Bryony. 'Me and Emma can do it.'

'No, no! I'm on it!' insisted Mum. 'Just as soon as I get the washing in. Won't be a sec!'

She dashed outside and while they were waiting Bryony poured two glasses of squash.

'Gosh, your mum's really busy,' Emma said.

'Wedding on Saturday,' Bryony explained, handing Emma a drink. 'And Mum's doing the flowers – as you might have guessed!'

Bryony loved that her mum was so busy with work again. After her dad had died last year, there was a time when she wondered if Mum would ever touch a flower again. But here she was, up to her eyes in ivy! And Mum might only have a couple of days to make all the *hundreds* of roses and grape hyacinths into the most beautiful bouquets, but

Bryony knew that she would somehow weave her magic . . .

Just then there was a knock at the open door and Abi, Bryony's favourite riding instructor at Seaview, came in clutching a clipboard and pen. Abi had been busy too, arranging Saturday's gymkhana.

'Hi, Abi!' said the girls.

'Hello, girls,' replied Abi. 'How's the gymkhana practice going?'

'Really well,' answered Bryony, but Emma across the table stayed conspicuously silent.

'How's Piggy, Emma?' Abi asked.

'Um, mostly peckish,' Emma sighed.

'But he's moving much more now,' Bryony chipped in. 'And he can go like a rocket when he *feels* like it!'

'Well, Red will show him what's what, I'm sure,' Abi smiled.

Bryony felt a thrill to hear Abi talk so highly of Red, especially after Georgina's hurtful comments yesterday. But she didn't want to boast in front of Emma as she'd hate to hurt her feelings. So she just gave Abi a little nod back instead.

'Anyway,' said Abi. 'I just popped round to

ask how your mum's doing with the gymkhana bunting, Bryony.'

'Um, fine! I mean – great – she's – yes!' squeaked Bryony.

'So shall I take it now, then?' Abi asked.

'No! Err . . .' Bryony took a deep breath to try and stop a gigantic blush. 'The thing is, it's not *quite* finished,' she went on. 'So anyway – aren't these flowers lovely?'

Bryony picked up a rose and gave it a big sniff as Abi and Emma looked on, confused.

Abi nodded slowly.

'Err, yeah – really pretty. About the bunting. I'll need it by tomorrow. Could you tell your mum?' she asked.

'Totally!' cried Bryony. 'So was that all you came for?'

'Yep,' Abi answered. 'That was it. Are you okay, Bry? You're looking a bit on edge.'

'I'm fine!" gasped Bryony. 'Brilliant, in fact. I . . . yeah – totally great!'

'Right,' said Abi. She looked puzzled and headed off with a wave.

'Bye!' called Emma.

'Yes!' gasped Bryony. 'Um, totally!'

When the girls were alone, 'Bry,' whispered Emma, 'what was *that* all about?'

'What?'

'You couldn't wait to get Abi out of the door!'

'Oh . . .' Bryony sighed. 'Was it *that* obvious?'

Emma nodded. 'A bit.'

Bryony frowned. 'Okay, so the bunting for the gymkhana – *I've* been doing it instead of Mum. Mum doesn't even know Abi wanted her to make it because I never passed on the message.'

'Why not?' asked Emma.

Raising her eyebrows, Bryony looked around the room, gesturing at the forest of flowers before them.

'Oh, yeah, she's flat-out busy,' said Emma. 'That was really kind of you, Bry. So . . . how much have you actually *done*?'

Bryony's face fell. Plodding to the dresser, she opened a drawer and pulled out a measly string of bunting. A total of five lopsided flags.

'It's taken me *hours*,' Bryony groaned, 'and look how much fabric I've still got left!' The drawer was crammed with creased fabric still not even cut into the right shape.

'I *hate* bunting,' said Bryony flatly. 'It's harder than you think, sewing it on straight. It keeps jiggling about, making me go wrong! Plus, I jammed up Mum's sewing machine so now I'll have to do it by *hand*.'

With that, she heard her mum heading back in so she stuffed the string of bunting into the drawer.

'I'll do some more tonight,' Bryony whispered. 'I've just been so busy with gymkhana stuff, you know?'

'And helping me with Piggy,' Emma whispered back. 'Sorry.'

'No, I'd rather help you than make bunting any day,' said Bryony.

As the girls ate lunch, surrounded by flowers, Bryony relaxed a bit. It felt like a flower fairy picnic in the kitchen and Bryony thought her mum definitely looked the part in a long frilly skirt and floaty blouse.

These were not the clothes she usually worked in, but because she'd been so busy recently, the washing had stacked up and her normal everyday work clothes (mostly dungarees and striped tops!) had only just come in from the washing line.

Bryony loved her mum's wispy brown hair too, tied up in its usual loose bun. Threaded into it today was a small pale yellow rose. Its stalk, thought Bryony, must have broken off too high so it couldn't be used in the bouquets.

'Hey, let's find more stray flowers,' said Bryony, 'and make Blueberry a flower fairy hairband!'

The cat, who'd been snoozing on the window seat, opened an eye as the girls measured his head with a bit of ribbon.

'I don't think he'll like it,' Emma giggled.

'He will!' snorted Bryony as the cat closed his eye again and huffed.

So, in between mouthfuls of crisp hot pasty, the girls got fairy hairband-making! Halfway through, Blueberry woke up and repositioned himself under the kitchen table, waiting for falling crumbs of pasty. Bryony suddenly wondered if Lavender's ginger cat, Marmalade, had ever had a flower hairband made for *him* by Lavender when she was a girl.

'Look, Berry!' said Bryony finally. 'This is for you!'

She popped the finished garland on the grumpy cat's head, pronouncing him 'King of the Fairies'.

He whacked it off with a swift swipe of the paw and flounced off, clearly offended.

'Told you,' grinned Emma, and Bryony laughed. 'Mr Grump!'

After they'd eaten their pasty and toast, Bryony's mum brought them over some ice cream. 'Miss Pigeon dropped in earlier,' smiled Mum, 'with a boxful of groceries I hadn't asked for. Anyway, in it was this ice cream! So kind of her,' she added. 'It was almost as if she *knew* I was busy and hadn't had the time to shop today.'

'Ooooooo,' giggled the girls in a spooky voice. Miss Pigeon, the old lady who ran the post office and store (that sold almost *everything*!), was always saying she had this 'amazing talent' of being able to see the future . . .

'And she popped in that needle and thread too!' said Mum, pointing to them on the dresser. 'Which I *certainly* don't need when I've got a perfectly good sewing machine!'

The girls exchanged glances.

'Bunting . . .' mouthed Emma, and Bryony gave a gulp. This was not the first time Miss Pigeon had got her predictions spot on!

Mum looked at the flowers and checked her watch.

'Goodness!' she said. 'Is that the time? Bryony, I thought you were meeting the others at two?'

'She is,' answered Josh, heading through the back door. He'd been out practising rugby moves with Finn.

'Wait! Don't tell me you're eating ice cream?' said Josh. 'That's no good for riders in training! I mean, bananas, sure . . . blueberries and . . . fish! Brain food – that's what you lot should be eating. Me and Finn were talking about it this morning and I decided that between now and Saturday's gymkhana the team must only eat high-energy-super-brain foods if you want to do well.'

The girls agreed. Then Bryony pointed out that it was a shame to waste the ice cream already in their bowls so they polished it off, as fast as Piggy would, before Josh could confiscate it. (And then probably eat it himself! Bryony thought.)

'And I've been reading up on relaxing before big events too,' Josh went on. 'Lavender oil's meant to be good for that.'

'Oh!' said Bryony. At the mention of lavender, her thoughts once again turned to Lavender Jones.

'Josh, have you seen Gramps today?' asked Bryony.

'Nope,' replied Josh. 'Why?'

'So there's this old lady,' said Bryony.

'What lady?' asked Mum, heading over for a flower.

'She's called Lavender Jones,' Bryony replied. 'Me and Emma met her this morning. She used to live in the old lighthouse a really long time ago.'

'There's something sad about her,' Emma chipped in. 'She's come back to say goodbye to the place.'

'But her heart's still here, I'm sure!' said Bryony. 'I just get the feeling she doesn't really want to leave. And I wondered if Grandpa might remember her from when he was young, or if he knew her story.'

'My dad said a lighthouse keeper died there once, rescuing a fishing boat,' said Emma.

'And I wondered if it had been *Lavender's* dad,' said Bryony. 'But I didn't want to ask in case it *had* been and then that would really upset her. Because I know what it's like when—'

Bryony stopped. She had nearly said 'when your dad dies', but she didn't want to upset Mum either.

Mum bent over and stroked Bryony's hair.

'You're very kind,' she said with a smile. 'But I'm afraid Gramps won't know her as he didn't live here as a child.'

'Oh, yeah,' replied Bryony. 'I forgot.'

'You forgot?' Mum winked, looking at the flowers on the table. 'Then you'll need one of these!' And she handed Bryony a small blue forget-me-not.

'Yes, that's *exactly* what I need!' grinned Bryony, suddenly remembering it was time to pick up Red as he would have just finished his riding lesson.

Bryony grabbed her riding hat. 'Em, you get Piggy, I'll get Red, then meet us at the stables just before two and we'll head to the field with the others. I'd like to do more jumping this afternoon, Josh.'

Josh nodded back. 'I've made a gymkhana countdown timetable.' He proudly took it out of his pocket.

'And we've still got an awful lot to get through,' he said. 'So let's go!'

Chapter 6

'We were here first.'

Georgina Brook looked determined as she sat, very upright, on Beau.

'Hey, that's not fair!' frowned Josh.

'Oh, well . . .' smirked Georgina, '*deal with it*!'

It was two o'clock and Bryony and the others had just gathered at the field – only to find it being used by Georgina and *her* relay team!

Josh stood his ground. 'We booked it out on the Seaview noticeboard,' he said. 'You've already had it way more than anyone.'

'Well, *we're* here now,' Georgina scoffed. 'So either stay and watch us do everything brilliantly, or go and find somewhere else!'

Georgina's friends started to laugh as they sat on their ponies looking smug. Her team were calling themselves 'The Fabulous Five', and by the way they'd been bragging round the stables they clearly thought they'd win everything on Saturday.

Either side of Georgina were Camilla and Eloise. And today George and Max, two snooty boys, were with them too. Georgina's pony was standing slightly in front of the others. Bryony guessed that she'd set herself up as leader.

'Move!' said Georgina, glaring at Bryony and the others.

'You tell them, Georgie,' Camilla giggled.

'Huh!' grinned Eloise. 'I don't know why they're even *bothering*.'

Bryony felt her body stiffen. She knew she needed to try and stay relaxed or Red would pick up on her mood and then he'd get stressed too. Bryony *always* put Red before herself.

But she found staying calm really hard when Georgina was being so nasty. Georgina had this knack of making you feel that things were *your* fault, when you knew, deep down, that they couldn't be.

Already Bryony was finding herself wondering if her team had, somehow, got it wrong and maybe it *wasn't* their turn in the field.

Then her mind flicked back to the first time she'd ever visited Georgina's house. Bryony had been keen to make friends in Brook Dale, and had taken along a tin of blueberry muffins she'd baked. But she'd barely stepped through the door when the tin had been 'accidentally' hit out of her hands by Georgina Brook, and the lovely muffins smashed to bits. At once Bryony had felt silly. Like it was all her fault. And Georgina had said nothing to persuade her it wasn't, even though Bryony had been holding the tin really carefully . . .

Bryony looked at Georgina's upturned nose and her pale doll-like features. She mustn't let Georgina ruin this gymkhana for her and Red. Or for her friends and brother who'd been working so hard for it.

'Come on, guys,' Bryony said to the others. As much as she didn't want to back away, she decided to be the better person and leave. Besides, all this arguing was wasting valuable practice time.

She turned around and the others followed,

trotting out of the field behind her, with Josh on his bike. Bryony glanced back over her shoulder to see Georgina looking triumphant. She always had to get her own way.

'So what's the plan now?' Alice asked.

'More practice,' said Hari. 'But where?'

'How about the fields behind my house?' suggested Emma.

'Do you think we'd be allowed there, Em?' asked Bryony. They were lovely flat fields, perfect for practising in, but they *did* belong to the Brooks.

'I'll ask my dad,' answered Emma.

'Yeah, but we won't have jumps.' Josh frowned, still cross about Georgina's group getting all the equipment. 'Hey, why don't we sneak to Georgina's outdoor school and use that while she's in *our* field?' he said.

Georgina had her own private manège just behind the stables at her house.

'We'd better not,' replied Bryony, although she was quite tempted by Georgina's state-of-the-art outdoor school. 'We might get into trouble. Let's just use one of her fields – if Emma's dad thinks it's okay. Forget the jumps, I'll be fine doing other things.'

'We could practise our starts and turns,' suggested Hari. 'Daffy needs—'

But Hari stopped, spotting Daffodil eyeing up the fishmonger's hat as he passed with a bucketful of fish. Saul Salmon grinned, having also seen. She'd had it off his head last week too!

'Daffodil . . .' Hari's voice was firm and Daffy's ears drooped to the side.

'I should think so too, young lady,' said Hari, even more sensitive about her playful ways after what Georgina had said yesterday. 'Less pranks and more concentration, please!'

Alice seemed very up for an afternoon of what Bryony had termed 'doing other things'.

'I could practise plaiting Princess Perla's mane for the dressage event!' she beamed. She was determined to pamper her rumble-tumble princess to the nines.

'*Or*,' said Finn, 'you could practise your dressage test. I've brought a very informative book along to show you. It's got masses of useful information on all aspects of dressage, including what they look for in a flawless rising trot.'

Alice sighed. 'I suppose so,' she said. 'Yes, you're probably right.'

'Hey, Alice, we'll plait tomorrow,' Bryony promised, 'when we get the ponies ready for Saturday. You could help me with Red's mane too, if you don't mind?'

'*Mind?*' squealed Alice. 'Of course I don't mind! The more to plait the merrier – it's a deal!'

Instead of dwelling on what had just happened with Georgina, Bryony now told Finn about the lighthouse 'ghost'.

'Turns out she's a sweet old lady called Lavender Jones.'

'What?!' cried Finn. 'But the *stars*? They were wrong?'

'It looks like it,' replied Bryony. 'Because ghosts drift *through* doors but Lavender has a key as she lived there long ago.'

Her friends were keen to find out more, so the girls shared the other snippets they knew.

'Wow! Her dad was a *lighthouse keeper*?' gasped Hari. 'That must have been so cool!'

'But my dad told me a lighthouse keeper died,' said Emma, 'rescuing a boat.'

'Except we don't know if it was him,' added Bryony. 'She did say it wasn't a working lighthouse when they lived there, I think.'

'Well, I have some info, too,' said Finn. 'Last night I told Dad about the shadow we saw and he said that the Stormy Point Lighthouse had been on TV just the other week.'

'Wait! There was a *programme*?' cried Bryony. 'Did your dad watch it? That could answer so many questions! For one, it might explain why she left Brook Dale. And maybe why she's come back now!'

'Yeah, I think Dad did watch it,' answered Finn. 'But last night he was on his way out so didn't say anything else. I'd guess it was a programme about building, though, as that's the kind of thing he watches.' Finn's dad was a builder and they lived in an unusual underground house set into one of the hills.

'A programme about building . . . ?' Bryony muttered to herself as they continued on up the leafy lane. Maybe, she thought, the lighthouse was going to be repaired.

Bryony's brain was now whirring in a most

Ebony Swann kind of way. This was all getting more and more interesting! Not only had Lavender come back to Brook Dale, but she'd come just after the lighthouse had been on TV. Might the two be – somehow – linked?

'Hmmm . . .' Bryony muttered to herself. 'The plot thickens . . .'

*

They arrived at Brook Dale Manor and Bryony looked around. As she had expected, the place looked gorgeous – from the elegant curve of the white sweeping driveway to the perfect symmetry of the house. The lawns were velvet-soft and the flower beds so neat, filled with straight purple tulips and large pink frilly peonies. Emma's dad had clearly been working very hard.

The Brooks' stables flowed out behind the house, and their many fields fanned out all around it. Georgina's father, Austin Brook, was a lawyer so had lots of money to spend on his estate. When he wasn't in London, he loved playing lord of the Brook Dale Manor – which had been in his family for generations. Georgina's mother, Arabella, although the most friendly of the Brooks, also liked the place to look just so.

They went around the back, not even daring to *breathe* on Georgina's posh outdoor school.

'Why does she want to take *our* practice field,' frowned Josh. 'When her stables are so cool?' The school was equipped with all the latest in pony-riding luxury.

'Probably just to wind us up!' said Hari.

They found Emma's dad, who said it should be okay to borrow a field as long as they kept a low profile, and suggested they use the one that backed onto Gardener's Cottage.

Bryony loved Emma's cottage. It was small but very cosy. She especially loved sleepovers in Emma's pretty bedroom, where a family of squirrels sometimes sunned themselves on her window ledge, or peeped in guiltily with a stolen acorn in their paws!

There were no signs of squirrels this afternoon, though, as the ponies were put through their paces. The clip-clopping of the hooves must have sent them all packing!

When they'd gone through their relays and

a few fun games, they practised their rising trots. Red didn't seem tired after his lunchtime lesson at all.

Halfway through the afternoon, Bryony's grandpa showed up to ask Emma's dad about cucumber pruning. He was having a problem with thin cucumbers down on the allotment.

'Bryony! Josh!' Grandpa waved from Emma's garden and the twins went over to see him.

'How's it going?' asked Grandpa. He stroked Red's glossy muzzle and Red gave a happy whinny.

'Really well!' replied Bryony. The afternoon had got better and better!

'Can you stay?' asked Josh. 'I need a hand with timing the ponies.'

Grandpa looked very pleased to be asked. 'Well, I am a dab hand with a stopwatch so – of course!' he smiled.

They carried on practising and Grandpa was a great help timing – and fussing the ponies! Bryony and Alice were both entered in the dressage on Saturday, so Hari wrote out the dressage letters on bits of paper and stuck them around the fence. Then Grandpa called out the test for Bryony, while Josh did the same for Alice further up the field.

'That's the way!' called Grandpa as Red walked from one letter to another. But Bryony knew she had to sharpen her turns if Red was to do as well as he deserved. She had always loved dressage and done rather well in it at her old riding stables back in the city. But Seaview took dressage more seriously than Park Lodge had, and the children here were so on it! Peak Point and White Cliff were likely to be the same and Bryony knew that she had to raise her game. She didn't have Alice's neatness, or Hari's ferocious grit. And even though Hari could be scarily competitive, Bryony needed to listen and learn from her. Hari had done dressage on her old pony last year and knew what the judges would be looking for.

'You need to smooth out those transitions from trot to canter, Bry,' said Hari as Bryony finished her test.

Bryony nodded. 'I know.' She patted Red's neck. 'Let's go again!'

Bryony and Red practised and practised, and she could feel Red improving all the time. He was starting to keep a good steady rhythm, perfectly in tune with Bryony's, and he needed no reminding to keep on going.

'Bravo!' called Grandpa as Red trotted past absolutely faultlessly. Bryony looked and felt nice and relaxed, not pushing up from her shoulders, but allowing Red's momentum and her legs to push her up.

Over the past few months, since she'd first sat on Red's back, she'd often got the feeling that he was making progress as she polished and refined his movements. But riding him every day made tracking his progress difficult. Now, though, it was clear, as he performed for Grandpa, that the little pony had come on in leaps and bounds!

'Neat work,' said Hari, when Bryony brought him to a halt.

'I'll second that!' Grandpa nodded, and Bryony smiled back, glowing with happiness.

'Thanks!'

They'd finished for the day and when Red had had a drink she stroked the little white star on his forehead.

'My beautiful little star,' Bryony whispered. Her

dad used to call *her* his little star. If only Dad could come to the gymkhana, thought Bryony, he'd be so proud of them both.

Red's eyes met hers. 'Trust me,' she whispered as she felt his warm breath. 'We'll show Georgina how special you are. We'll show *everyone* . . .'

Chapter 7

'Oh no . . .' groaned Bryony.

'What?' gasped Emma as they trotted out of the field together.

'I've just remembered my "fun" night ahead,' sighed Bryony. 'The bunting . . .'

Emma quickly offered to lend a hand.

'Are you *sure*?' asked Bryony. Emma nodded back brightly.

'Oh, Em – thanks so much. You're a lifesaver! And would it be pushing it,' Bryony grinned, 'to ask your dad if you can stay for a sleepover too? The bunting might well take all night!'

'Yep, knowing my sewing, it probably will!' giggled Emma.

The girls parted at Seaview and Bryony rode Red in to settle him down for the night. She adored the dreamy smell of straw and polish that greeted her every time she crossed the stable yard. It was familiar and comforting and it always made her smile.

Bryony mucked out Red's stable and took the wheelbarrow outside. The stables were buzzing with gymkhana chatter . . .

'I've heard,' said eight-year-old Toby Halfpenny, 'that Peak Point all ride ponies that look like *actual* dragons.'

'Yep, me too,' said his friend, Arthur Dobbs. 'And some of them breathe *actual* fire!'

'That's nonsense,' said Tabitha Tibberthwaite-Browne, who was seven and super-confident.

'Mummy says Cockledore are "Wet weekends" and Nettleton are "Right little grump-bags". She says we *should* win – but only if we focus, focus, FOCUS!'

Tabby waved to Bryony and Bryony waved back. 'Hi, Tabby!'

Returning to Red, Bryony giggled to herself at the thought of Tabby's mum. Belinda-Jayne Tibberthwaite-Browne was really pushy. She was meant to be getting some polo shirts printed for all the Seaview Stables supporters.

'*Except*,' Bryony quietly confided in Red, 'Alice was told by Toby, who was told by Amy, who was told by Hari, who was told by Aisha, whose mum is a friend (but not *really*) of Belinda's, that although they'll just have the Seaview logo on the back, they're *all* going to have a very large picture of Tabby's pony (called Tiberius after a powerful Roman Emperor) on the front!'

Red looked at her, blinked and gave a little snort.

'I know!' chuckled Bryony. 'Hilarious!''

She now gave Red a good brush down as they'd been out and about all day and his coat was looking quite dusty.

'Good boy,' she said, as he stood very still, allowing her to get out all the tangles. Red's eyes were shining. They always shone for Bryony. But he was standing with one leg off the ground and Bryony knew he was sleepy.

She finished up and gave his ears a little tickle.

'All done then!'

Red followed Bryony across the stable and

waited as she topped up his water trough and re-filled his hay net with sweet fresh hay.

As he started to munch his tasty supper, Bryony lovingly patted him goodnight. But before she could leave, someone appeared at the door. It was Abi.

'Hi, Abi!' said Bryony. But Abi was frowning.

'Is everything okay?' Bryony asked.

'Not *exactly*,' replied Abi. She sounded oddly abrupt. Usually Abi was very laid-back.

'Are you needing to lock up?' Bryony said. She checked her watch. 'Gosh! I didn't realise it was this late. I must have got carried away brushing Red.'

'No, *actually* I'm glad you're still here,' said Abi curtly, 'or I wouldn't have caught you before your trip.'

'My trip?' repeated Bryony, now frowning slightly too. Bryony had no trips planned . . .

'But, Abi, I—'

'Anyway,' Abi cut in, 'I just wanted to say, well, it would have been polite to have just told me yourself.'

'Told you? Told you *what*?' Bryony gasped. This was all really puzzling!

'I mean, you could have said at lunchtime,' continued Abi, 'when I called round asking about the bunting.'

'Said what?' cried Bryony. 'Sorry, but, Abi – I just . . . I don't understand!'

'That you were going away for the weekend,' replied Abi. 'And pulling out of the gymkhana *last minute*. Lucky I found out before I got all the programmes printed.'

Bryony felt her jaw drop.

'No, Abi, I think you've . . .' she began. But Abi was already heading off.

'Anyway,' Abi called back over her shoulder, 'as you're not going to be around I've put Sara Wells on Red instead – and she's thrilled.'

*

For a moment Bryony could hardly take it in. But then the penny dropped. From what Abi had just said, she was no longer in the gymkhana!

She ran outside. The place was much quieter save for one or two keen beans still about. She saw Tabitha Tibberthwaite-Browne and her mother polishing Tiberius's saddle for Saturday. Sara Wells, thought Bryony with a sudden pang, would be doing that for Red now!

Abi was heading back to her office on the other side of the yard. As Bryony hurried after her, she passed Juno's open top door. Georgina's friend, Camilla, was inside settling Juno for the night. But wait! Georgina Brook was in there too, which was most unusual as Georgina *never* just waited around for anyone . . .

'Abi!' cried Bryony, catching her up. 'Sorry! But what trip am I meant to be going on?'

'To see your aunt,' replied Abi.

'*My aunt?*' frowned Bryony. She hadn't seen her aunt for *ages* and they'd no plans to visit!

In the corner of her eye, Bryony saw Georgina edge into the corner of Juno's stable. It was like she didn't want to be spotted.

'Th-the thing is, Abi,' Bryony continued, 'I'm not going to visit my aunt – especially this weekend. I'd *never* miss a gymkhana, or pull out last minute and let everyone down.'

'But I was told,' said Abi, 'that you'd definitely not be here.'

'Told? By who?' Bryony asked. But suddenly the penny dropped . . .

'By Georgina,' said Abi, just as Bryony had suspected!

'I saw Georgina earlier,' Abi went on, 'and she told me then.'

Abi seemed to have no idea that Georgina was still hanging about. *Gloating with Camilla, no doubt!* thought Bryony. That had to be why she was here at all. To make mischief and spread lies.

'Georgina has made a mistake,' said Bryony. She was trying her best to sound calm, even though she was fuming. 'Why don't we just ask her? She's in with Camilla now.'

Abi looked surprised. 'Oh, really?' she said. 'Um, Georgina!' called Abi, stepping across to Juno's door, the top part of which was open.

'Georgina, are you in there? Can I have a word, please?' called Abi, and Georgina's face appeared.

'A word? Um . . .' Georgina checked her watch.

'Oh, goodness, is that the time?!' she cried. 'Sorry, Abi – I didn't realise it was so late. I really have to get home!'

She opened the stable door and stepped out swiftly, about to head off across the yard.

'It won't take a minute,' Abi said.

'But Daddy's home from the city,' replied Georgina, 'and Mummy is having a dinner party. They would both rather I wasn't late, so sorry.'

Georgina sounded as confident as ever, but Bryony could just detect a nervous look in those icy blue eyes. Georgina started to walk away, her white-blonde ponytail glistening with pink as the setting sun hung in the sky.

'I only need you for a moment,' insisted Abi. 'This is important.'

Georgina stopped in her tracks and turned around.

'Bryony tells me,' Abi said, 'that she's not away this weekend.'

Georgina put on a look of surprise and Bryony shook her head. Why could nobody ever see through her?

'Really?' said Georgina. 'Oh right. I could have sworn I heard Bryony tell Emma earlier that the whole family were off to stay with her aunt. But clearly I must have been mistaken.'

'I never—' began Bryony, but Georgina gave a gasp.

'Gosh, Abi!' she cried. 'Have you done the

gymkhana programmes? Is it too late to put Bryony back in?'

'Of course it isn't!' Bryony frowned.

But Abi suddenly looked thoughtful . . .

'The thing *is*,' said Abi, looking at Bryony now, 'I've literally *just* sent someone off to deliver Cockledore's and Nettleton's programmes. And Sara Wells has been told too and she's really excited about riding Red.'

Bryony liked Sara, who had riding lessons on Red as part of his livery deal. But naturally, *she* longed to ride Red in the gymkhana *herself*. That was what all the practice had been for.

Feeling huge hot tears welling up in her eyes, Bryony rushed across, closed the top part of Red's door for the night, then hurried away past Abi and Georgina.

'Bryony!' called Abi, but Bryony started to run and didn't stop until she was out on the lane. She had never ridden her own pony in a gymkhana before, but had wanted to for so long! And Red was so special. And preparing him for Saturday had felt like an absolute dream.

Now Georgina Brook had snatched that dream away.

Chapter 8

'Are you all right, my dear?' somebody said and Bryony turned to see who it was. Lavender Jones was standing beside the bench Bryony was sitting on, the old lighthouse silhouetted on the cliffs behind her.

'Um . . .' Was she all right? Bryony wasn't quite sure. Her eyes were stinging but at least she'd stopped crying.

'I – yes,' Bryony heard herself say. 'I just . . . I've just been thinking.'

'Ah, I see,' Lavender nodded. 'A very good spot for clearing your mind, this old prom.'

Bryony suddenly became aware of the waves crashing onto the sand down below. How long had she been there? She'd lost all track of time.

Some of the cottages on the hills around the cove had their lights on now. But it wasn't yet totally dark so Bryony supposed she couldn't have been sitting there for as long as it felt.

'Could I join you?' asked Lavender.

'Oh, um, yes,' replied Bryony. She budged up to make room and Lavender sat down.

Bryony didn't feel like chatting, though having company felt oddly nice. She waited for Lavender to ask her what was wrong. But Lavender didn't. She didn't say anything. She just gazed at the swirly purple-blue sky which looked as if it had just been poured from an ink pot.

The ebb and flow of the waves, like the trotting of hooves, was steady and sure. It had purpose. Lavender, thought Bryony, was right about this spot. Her mind, she now realised, felt a lot clearer than when she'd first raced up here from the stables, panting and cross and tearful.

'So . . .' said Bryony after a while, 'I was meant to be riding Red on Saturday in The Three Coves Gymkhana. But something's . . . something's happened, and now it looks like I can't.'

'Ahh, I see,' said Lavender quietly. 'That's sad.'

Bryony nodded, tucking a stray curl behind her ear. As she did, she thought of Red's adorable little kiss curl and his rich toffee-coloured coat. Tomorrow she had planned to give him a bath to make sure he looked his best for the dressage. Alice was going to help her plait his mane too. Most likely Sara would want to do all that now.

Bryony sighed. She was being rubbish company. But Lavender didn't seem to mind. She appeared to be happy enough gazing out at the splashes of moonlight on the sea.

'Did *you* ever sit on this bench,' asked Bryony, 'when you lived in the lighthouse as a girl?'

'Indeed I did,' Lavender nodded. 'Sometimes. I sat with friends and we gossiped and swung our legs. Or I came by myself and just sat, and thought . . . like you.'

It was starting to get chilly. Bryony blew on her hands and put them into her hoodie pocket. 'Oh!' She pulled out a crumpled pink and white striped bag with a couple of sherbet lemons left inside that she'd bought from the post office last week.

'Would you like one?' she asked Lavender.

'Oh, thank you!' Lavender smiled. 'Goodness, this takes me back. A sherbet lemon from the post office – still the same pretty bags as when I was girl, you know! Father loved sherbet lemons so very much.'

Bryony thought that Ebony Swann would be all over that snippet of information like a rash. And Bryony would normally be too. But right now it was just nice to sit beside Lavender and eat sweets.

'Who runs the post office now?' asked Lavender.

'A lady called Miss Pigeon,' replied Bryony.

'Not Eliza Pigeon? Well, I never!' gasped Lavender. 'I went to school with Eliza Pigeon. Is Dorothea Parsley still round these parts too? Now *she* would have sweets galore! And string and crayons and feathers and stones all stuffed in her desk at school. A right little hoarder old Dotty was back then!'

'Yes, she's still here too,' Bryony nodded. 'She lives in a strawberry-pink cottage in town.'

'Do Eliza and Dotty still fight like cats and dogs?' Lavender asked with a grin.

'Yes,' answered Bryony. 'Especially over who makes the best jam.'

'Ahh,' nodded Lavender. 'That doesn't surprise me. They used to fight over everything! I must look them up before I leave. Although if they still squabble, maybe separately . . .'

Bryony was starting to feel a tiny bit better now. Talking to Lavender was helping. 'So, did Brook Dale have a riding stable when you lived here?' she asked.

'Yes, it was called Land's End Stables then,' said Lavender, 'and it stood where Seaview is now.'

'I could take you to see Seaview before you leave – i-if you'd like?' Bryony offered. 'Red likes you. I could tell the minute you met. He's very choosy about who he lets tickle him between the ears.' Red was a great judge of character.

'He's so dear!' said Lavender. 'Have you owned him for long?'

'Since last summer,' replied Bryony. 'My grandpa helped me buy him – and I wanted . . .' She stopped, feeling another pang of sadness coming on. Bryony waited until its sting had numbed a little, then taking a deep breath, she continued.

'. . . and I wanted to thank Grandpa for all he's

done by doing well on Red in the gymkhana. But now Georgina Brook has ruined everything!'

'Georgina Brook?' repeated Lavender, looking suddenly thoughtful. 'There were Brooks living here when I was a girl too. Must be her old relatives,' she said. 'Algernon Brook, who owned the big house then, was some sort of lawyer, I think. Very snooty he was, and he'd be – let's think . . . Georgina's great-grandfather on her father's side.'

'So snooty runs in the family then,' said Bryony glumly.

'Georgina used to own Red too,' she explained. 'But she hated him. Oh, and hated me more – and still does. And she's been so mean today!' And before she knew it, everything came tumbling out. About the insults, about Georgina swiping their practice field, and finally about the worst thing of all – the lie that Georgina had told Abi about Bryony visiting her aunt!

'And that's why I'm out of the gymkhana,' Bryony sighed.

Lavender sat thoughtfully. 'That does sound very mean,' she said. 'And I would be as cross as you. But when I was girl and others had been mean and got me all angry inside, my father, who was wise, used to say to me: "Lavender, just you have courage and be kind, then you can hold your head high! Courage to do what you think is right, even if it doesn't always make you popular, and kindness in how *you* behave *in spite* of others."'

Bryony mulled this over for a minute.

'I think I'm mostly kind,' she said. 'And I was definitely courageous last summer.'

Lately though, her courage, she felt, had been wavering as Georgina continually heaped insults on Red. Bryony had hoped these would stop when Georgina had got Beau, but they hadn't.

'It, um, sounds like your father was very nice,' said Bryony. 'My dad would have probably said something like that too.'

'Would have?' Lavender asked her gently.

Bryony nodded. 'He died. Last year, in January. More than a year ago now, but . . . sometimes it seems like just the other day. Except Dad doesn't know that some things have changed and I find it – well, weird that he doesn't. Like he doesn't know I've no more baby teeth to lose because that last one finally fell out last June. And he doesn't know what my new bedroom looks like. Or that my old watch broke and we had to buy another. I didn't want to because Dad had given me the old one but it just wouldn't tick again. And of course he doesn't know that I've got Red now. Dad painted our front door in the city red once, I remember. Red's coat reminds me of that door when the sun shines on it. And then it reminds me of Dad too.'

It was Lavender's turn to be quiet now. After a while she looked at Bryony.

'My father died when I was twelve,' she said. 'Mother and I weren't here when it happened. We were on our way to Australia to "make a new life" out there. My mother wanted a new life, you see, and she thought that I did too. But I was perfectly fine with the *old* one, and so was Father. I only wish I'd had the courage to tell her that . . .'

Bryony waited, as she got the feeling there was more. The mystery was starting to unravel, but all that she could think about now was how awful it must have been for Lavender having to leave her dad. Ebony Swann's mysteries didn't always have happy endings. But this felt really different. This wasn't pretend. Lavender Jones was a real person with real feelings.

'There had been posters everywhere,' Lavender went on, 'advertising this "exciting new life" far, far away in Australia. Mother and I spent weeks on board the ship taking us right across the world – we couldn't have travelled any further away. Almost forty days, if I remember rightly. It seemed like a whole lifetime! Our ship set off from Southampton bound for Sydney. But then, while we were travelling across, there was a terrible storm. Not out at sea where Mother and I were, but here in Brook Dale where my father was. Anyway, there was a fishing boat. My father tried to save it. He was so brave. And so kind. He did save it too. But the storm was too wild and from what I heard Father fell into the water. It was cold. Too cold. They rescued him finally but . . . it was too late.'

'Oh no!' gasped Bryony. So the lighthouse keeper that Emma had mentioned before – the one who'd died – *was* Lavender's dad!

'How – I mean – when did you find out?' asked Bryony, imagining how horrible it must have been.

'Not until we'd docked and set up life in Australia,' Lavender replied. 'It took a few months to track us down and then we received a letter. By then the funeral, it was all over. So I never got to say a proper goodbye to him.'

'How awful!' blurted Bryony. It must have been so terribly sad not having the chance to say goodbye. 'So what happened when you found out?' she continued. 'I-if you don't mind me asking?'

'No,' said Lavender, 'it was a long time ago. And time, as they say, is a very good healer, though things can never *quite* be the same.'

Bryony nodded. She knew what Lavender meant. She thought of the photo on the table by her bed taken on holiday the year before Dad got ill. He looked so happy. They all did, on holiday in France. There would always be three in family photos now. Her, Josh and Mum. She still always left a little space by her side though, whenever they had a new family photo. This was where Dad would have stood with his arm around her.

'Mother and I,' continued Lavender, 'couldn't afford to travel back. And what was the point anyway? So we stayed. We stayed in Australia and carried on with our lives – though it wasn't the "exciting new life" the posters had promised – not for many anyway. Eventually my mother met somebody new. But I thought of Father every day, and never stopped missing him. Anyway, years later I met a lovely Welsh man with dark hair and green eyes. Michael had also travelled out with some of his family when he was young. Eventually we got married and were very happy – for a jolly long time as well! It was when Michael died, two years ago, that I decided to finally come back. Not to here. I went to some of my husband's family still in Wales and have been living there for the last year. I couldn't bring myself to come back to Brook Dale, you see, until I felt ready to say goodbye to the place, and in doing that, say a proper goodbye to Father.'

'You feel ready to say goodbye *now*?' asked Bryony. 'Seeing as you've just come back?'

She was sure that Lavender didn't want to say goodbye. Sure that Brook Dale was still weaving its magic on her – and if she *let* it, it could be a place she felt she really belonged.

As if Lavender could read Bryony's mind, 'No,

dear, I think you've guessed right,' she replied. 'I don't feel ready to close the Brook Dale chapter. The truth is, something forced me back before I was ready to come.'

Bryony was just about to ask what that was when Lavender got to her feet.

'Brrr, it's getting awfully chilly,' she said, wrapping her cardigan around her. 'I'd best get back to my B&B.'

'Wait! Come to my house for supper!' suggested Bryony. Much better, she thought, than Lavender being by herself, especially after she'd recalled such a sad story.

'Grandpa's coming too – and hopefully Emma,' went on Bryony. 'And I could do with a hand making bunting.'

Bryony supposed she still had to get *that* done even though she'd never see it hung up. She definitely *wasn't* going to the gymkhana! She couldn't bear to just stand there and watch somebody else ride Red.

'If you're sure,' replied Lavender. 'I do love sewing! What's the bunting for?'

'The gymkhana,' sighed Bryony. 'And we – I mean – *they* need a lot.'

Chapter 9

'Mum, this is Lavender Jones,' said Bryony, stepping into the snug, lamp-lit kitchen. 'I mentioned at lunch – me and Emma met her at the lighthouse.'

'Ah, yes!' Mum smiled, putting down a flower and heading over to say hello.

'Pleased to meet you, Mrs May,' Lavender said. 'I hope you don't mind me just appearing like this.'

'I invited Lavender and Emma to supper,' explained Bryony.

'Well, the more the merrier, I say!' replied Mum, shaking Lavender's hand. 'But I'm sorry that you can't see the kitchen table for roses! I'm a florist, you see, and I'm currently doing the flowers for a wedding on Saturday.'

'I hope it's before the gymkhana,' piped up Josh, heading in from the lounge with Finn. At the mention of the word 'gymkhana', Bryony's heart hit her boots again. It had been on her mind all the way home, buzzing away in the background like a swarm of angry bees. But now the awful truth stung her again. She *wasn't* in the gymkhana. And now she had to tell everyone the news . . .

Just then, Grandpa appeared with Emma, who he'd met coming along the lane. Emma looked surprised at seeing Lavender in Bryony's kitchen.

'So!' chuckled Grandpa, looking at Bryony. 'How's my budding dressage champ, then?'

Bryony felt her shoulders slump and everyone's eyes on her face.

'A-about the gymkhana,' she said with a sigh. And she forced herself to tell them the whole story . . .

'What?! The little madam!' Grandpa cried. 'I can't *believe* Georgina would make up such a lie. I mean, missing the gymkhana for a weekend trip! As if you would!'

'There must be something we can do?' said Bryony's mum, but Bryony shook her head.

'My name isn't in the programme, Mum. And Abi said she'd sent them to White Cliff and Peak Point already.'

As everyone muttered on about Georgina, Grandpa took Bryony aside. 'Now don't you go getting too downhearted,' he said. 'Because we are going to sort this out! I'll think of something to get you back in that gymkhana. You and Red are a team and everyone knows it, eh?'

'Thanks, Gramps,' whispered Bryony. She wasn't sure he could but it was great to have him on her side.

'Chin up, for me!' Grandpa said and Bryony nodded back with a watery smile.

'Sure.'

Emma introduced Lavender to Grandpa, Josh and Finn by telling them the story of how she and Bryony met her earlier.

'So Piggy actually bolted,' said Emma. 'I've never seen him go so fast.'

'What happened?' asked Finn.

'Well,' replied Emma. 'He saw a tasty patch of grass!'

'Right! Tempting snacks gets him moving,'

nodded Josh. And whipping a notebook from his jeans' pocket, he was just about to note that useful fact down when Bryony saw him look at her and stop.

'Sorry, Bry,' Josh mumbled. 'I was just thinking . . . for, um, Saturday.' But without writing down a single thing, he quickly slipped the notebook back away.

'It's okay,' replied Bryony. 'I still want you all to do well.'

Mum made everyone a nice cup of tea, and as they sat round the table drinking it, Bryony decided it was probably time to come clean about the bunting too.

'Mum,' she said, looking rather sheepish, 'Abi asked me to ask you if you wouldn't mind making some bunting for the . . .' She hesitated, not wanting to say the word 'gymkhana' in case it set her off again, '. . . for *Saturday*,' she continued. 'But I decided not to ask you because you've been so busy and I thought I could make the bunting instead. Except it's been a *nightmare*. Why do flags have to have such impossibly straight sides? And if that wasn't bad enough, the sewing machine jammed up— But I'm sure it can be fixed! As for the bunting, though . . . I've hardly done any, and Abi is expecting it quite soon.'

'How soon?' asked Josh and Bryony felt herself blush.

'By tomorrow.'

She looked at her mother, but Mum didn't look cross. Instead she walked over and put her arms around Bryony, who breathed in Mum's familiar flowery smell.

'You haven't had a great day, have you, love?' Mum asked.

'Not the best.'

'Thank you for thinking of me,' said Mum. 'But the last thing I want is you worrying and getting yourself all tied up in knots.'

'It's your sewing machine that's tied up in knots,' groaned Bryony.

'Nothing that can't be sorted, I'm sure!' Grandpa winked. 'Let's see it.'

While he did that and the boys found some tools, Mum finished off the last of the bridesmaids' bouquets, and Bryony and Emma set to peeling the potatoes for tea.

'I'll help peel too,' Lavender said.

'But you're our guest!' Mum protested.

'And I'd like to be a *useful* one,' insisted Lavender. 'I've always loved cooking – especially baking, which I could easily do all day!'

'Me too,' said Bryony. 'My speciality is blueberry muffins. And my cat is called that too.' The fat, grumpy silver-grey cat had taken rather a liking to Lavender, it seemed, curling round and round her legs.

'Gosh, Berry,' said Bryony, looking down into his fluffy, squashed-looking face. 'Aren't *you* the friendly one tonight?'

'He doesn't usually like people,' Emma whispered to Lavender, in case the cat heard and took offence.

'Really?' whispered Lavender, and Emma nodded back.

Bryony was glad Berry was being friendly and hoped that Lavender was feeling welcome. All this gymkhana drama had made Bryony forget that Lavender had business of her own in Brook Dale. She'd come to say a final goodbye to the place and to her dad, she'd said. Bryony knew that couldn't be easy. Especially as Lavender had admitted that something had forced her back now sooner than she would have come. Bryony began to wonder what that something was . . .

Wandering over to the recycling tub, she tipped in the potato peelings.

'Right!' said Mum, heading to wash her hands. 'Bridesmaids' flowers done so I can take over on supper.'

'Maybe we should start on that bunting, then?' Lavender suggested to Bryony.

'So you're still okay to help?' Bryony asked.

'Of course, dear,' Lavender smiled.

'And me!' nodded Emma.

'And us,' called Josh. 'As soon as this machine is fixed.'

'Oh, thanks, everyone,' Bryony replied. The more helpers the better.

She prised open the dresser drawer and unearthed a jumble of creased fabric of all colours and patterns. As Lavender set about ironing it, Bryony sat with Emma in the window seat.

'I've got so much to tell you, Em,' Bryony said, and she relayed all the snippets Lavender had told her about leaving for Australia, and her dad, with Emma gasping at all the sad parts.

'And if only I was in the gymkhana,' concluded Bryony. 'I bet Lavender would love to come and watch before she leaves.'

'I'm so sorry about all that,' said Emma. 'But now Abi knows that you're not away, maybe she'll ask Georgina – as it was her mistake – if she would share Beau with Sara, then you could be back in on Red.'

'Firstly,' said Bryony, 'since when does Georgina share? And secondly, it wasn't a mistake. Georgina deliberately wanted me out.'

'Oh yes,' said Emma glumly.

'I just needed everyone,' Bryony said, 'to see how great Red is – especially the Brooks. I wanted to be there for you and Piggy too.'

'I know,' Emma nodded. 'And we'll miss you.'

But, worst of all, Bryony couldn't bear the thought of letting Red down.

When the ironing was done, tea wasn't quite ready so the girls and Lavender started to draw out lots of triangular bunting flags on the now lovely flat fabric. Lavender taught them a good trick of using a cardboard template to do this as it was much quicker, so they cut up a cereal box, which was perfect.

Eventually, Grandpa and the boys came over. Grandpa had the sewing machine, which he popped down on the end of the kitchen table that hadn't yet been laid for supper.

'There you go,' he grinned. 'As good as new!'

'Oh, thanks, Gramps,' said Bryony.

'And *us*,' chipped in Josh. 'We helped too.'

'Finn had read a book on mechanisms,' explained Grandpa, 'which came in most useful!'

'Finn's read a book on *everything*,' grinned Josh.

'No,' corrected Finn. 'The one I wanted on quantum physics was out of the library so I haven't read *that* one yet.' Everyone laughed, and even Bryony managed a grin. The build-up to a gymkhana was always a special time and the last thing Bryony wanted to do was spoil it for everyone else by being gloomy.

With the sewing machine back in action, 'Project Bunting' could start in force. The children set up a little production line as tea cooked in the background, the smell making everyone hungry.

The girls started to cut out the triangular flags, which Josh and Finn arranged into nice colour combinations. Grandpa came next, passing each one to Lavender, who was a whizz on the sewing machine. While they did this, Bryony could see that Mum was keeping a close eye on the cottage pie bubbling away in the Aga. She wasn't the world's best cook, but it was obvious she was determined tonight's supper would be one of her best efforts. Thank goodness, though, Bryony suddenly thought, that Miss Pigeon had dropped by with all the ingredients earlier. Otherwise they'd be eating yesterday's leftovers – jelly and tuna bake sandwiches.

'It's ready, everyone!' Mum finally called, and swiftly clearing the table of fabric, they set it for supper and tucked in. The cottage pie was accompanied with spring greens, fresh from Grandpa's allotment.

'That'll perk you up, young Bryony!' Grandpa smiled.

Grandpa was right. Tea perked everyone up. As everyone chatted on, Bryony noticed how kind they were all being. No one mentioned the gymkhana once. She was very lucky to have such lovely friends and family, she thought.

Lavender really seemed at home in Plum Cottage now too, making Bryony believe even more strongly that she definitely belonged right here in Brook Dale.

She did hope Red was okay too. She had left him very abruptly, not wanting him to pick up on how upset she'd been for she knew that would have unsettled him too.

After everyone had had seconds of cottage pie, pudding was jam roly-poly. This was Bryony's favourite.

'My father used to love this pudding,' said Lavender. 'As well as sherbet lemons!' She winked at Bryony. 'Mother used to cook it on the little stove and we used to eat it up in the lighthouse watching the waves from the window.'

'Wow! That must have been really exciting,' said Finn.

Bryony was pleased that Lavender had just mentioned the lighthouse again without any prompting from her. She'd been increasingly sure that the recent programme about the lighthouse had had something to do with Lavender returning now. And here was the perfect chance – with Finn about too – for Bryony to gently bring it up again.

'Finn likes interesting buildings,' said Bryony. 'His dad, who's a builder, does too. In fact, Finn's dad watched a programme about your lighthouse, just the other week . . .'

Bryony watched to see how Lavender would respond to this. It just seemed too much of a coincidence that the programme had been on – and a week or so later here Lavender was. Ebony Swann said that coincidences were often clues in disguise.

Lavender nodded slowly. 'Yes, I saw that too,' she said. 'It was about a new nationwide venture to turn "old wrecks", as the presenter called them, into posh, upmarket hotels. I think the programme was called *Trash into Treasure*, or something very similar. Anyway . . . there it was. The Stormy Point Lighthouse – my old home. After all those years!'

'Gosh,' said Grandpa. 'That must have been a shock!'

'Well, I couldn't believe it!' Lavender replied. 'It felt like fate. Like the old lighthouse was somehow calling me back – its light was guiding me home. But then the programme's message began to sink in.'

'Which was?' prompted Bryony.

'Well,' Lavender replied, 'it seems a lawyer has been engaged to find out who owns the lighthouse, since it has been empty, the programme said, for many years. Of course, I lost touch with the place so I don't know if anyone lived in the lighthouse after my father. Anyway, it doesn't really matter, for the lawyer apparently has now declared that no deeds can be found.'

'Deeds?' asked Bryony.

'Official papers – err, documents,' Lavender replied, 'which have the owner's name on. The lawyer's search has drawn a blank. The original deeds cannot be found. A new deed has, therefore, been drawn up – and at precisely midday this coming Monday, this new deed will pass into the hands of Flaxen and Bloomfield, a group that already own a chain of posh hotels. By this time on Monday, they'll have bought the lighthouse in order to turn it into another of their hotels.'

'No!' cried Bryony. 'That means … *changing*

it. And I wonder who that lawyer is? I bet it's Mr Brook, Georgina's dad. He's home from London for something – Georgina told Abi. I bet it's for that!'

Lavender nodded. 'Perhaps – the programme didn't say. And yes, Flaxen and Bloomfield will probably change it a lot. I've done a bit of research and I'm sorry to say that if their past "transformations" are anything to go by, they may even flatten the old place completely and replace it with a huge posh box. It will probably soon be completely unrecognisable as what it has always *felt* like to me . . . home.'

'Dear me!' cried Grandpa.

'They can't!' shouted Bryony. 'Your old home isn't *trash* – it's a treasure!'

She might not have lived in Brook Dale all her life, but already Bryony felt a huge attachment to the lighthouse. It gave the headland such character. 'They can't sell it when it belonged to your dad – and now to you!' she said.

'Ah, but,' Lavender sighed, 'there's no proof that Father actually owned the place, you see.'

'But you have a key, don't you?' Emma chipped

in now. The Ebony Swann bug seemed to be catching. 'That's how you got in, right?'

Lavender nodded.

'So surely that must mean that you *own* it?' said Bryony. 'You *don't* have to go. You could stay – we'd fix it up. Paint it – my friends would all help!'

Mum patted Bryony's arm. 'It's not that easy, love.'

'You're so kind, Bryony,' Lavender said. 'But your mum is right. Me still having a key is no proof at all. Proof means *deeds* – proper bits of paper with my father's signature on. But this was all such a long time ago, and well . . . I've never seen such things.'

At this Lavender shook her head as if trying to jolt her thoughts back into the present.

'Now let's not worry about me any more, and finish off this bunting,' she said. They still had quite a lot of sewing left to do . . .

Bryony let the subject drop. But as they carried on with the bunting her brain was in a whirl. What if the deeds were still in Brook Dale? And if they were, where might they be? It would be like looking for a needle in a haystack. But worth it!

An hour or so later (thanks to Miss Pigeon bringing all that extra thread!), metres and metres of beautiful bunting filled the entire kitchen. It wove in and out of the flowers scattered about in buckets and jars, and went over the chairs and across the curtain poles. Then, as Blueberry batted the dangly flags coming over the table from the sewing machine, Lavender sewed on the very last one. 'All done!' she exclaimed with a satisfied nod.

'Hooray!' cheered everyone. It had been a real team effort.

'It's so pretty!' smiled Mum, admiring their hard work. Some of the flags had seaside things on, like shells and lighthouses and gulls. Others had cream flowers on a deep red background, and a couple of them were dotted with trotting ponies.

As Bryony picked out her favourite flag, she felt very proud of what they'd done – despite knowing she wouldn't be a part of the fun on Saturday.

The rest of the evening passed in a flash and it was soon time for Lavender to leave. As Bryony saw her out, she came face to face with her freshly-washed shirt and new riding jacket hanging on the back of the kitchen door ready for the gymkhana.

Bryony had saved up to buy the jacket herself, along with the matching cravat. As Red's livery fees were costing Mum and Grandpa such a lot, Bryony was determined to pay for as many of the other things she needed herself.

She'd bought the jacket second-hand from the riding shop in Nettleton just last week. Nettleton was bigger than Brook Dale or Cockledore and so stocked all the various riding clothes the stables in each town used. Coming home with the riding shop's fancy bag, Bryony had felt like she was walking on cloud nine! She didn't care that the jacket was second-hand, and despite saying 'dry clean only' on the label, Mum had earlier hand-washed it very carefully and now it was looking like new. Not, thought Bryony, that she'd get to wear it now . . .

She opened the door and walked Lavender down the path. The sky was a deep indigo blue and stars twinkled like glitter. This place really was quite magical.

'If only we could prove that lighthouse is still yours, then you could stay in Brook Dale for good,' said Bryony.

'Oh, Bryony,' smiled Lavender, taking her hands. 'That would be lovely. Really it would! You and your friends have reminded me how much I love it here. In fact, just today I found myself dreaming of opening up the lighthouse for everyone to come and enjoy it. I saw myself happily baking cakes, and people eating them, and drinking tea! A little lighthouse café, I thought, would be so lovely. That way I could share the place with everyone! The lighthouse as it is *now*, I mean, with its wonky walls and uneven winding stairs. Maybe give it a fresh lick of paint and fix up the old garden fence.'

'And maybe some flowers on the tables?' gasped Bryony. 'In the Lavender Lighthouse Tearoom, I mean! Daffodils in the spring, and *definitely* sea lavender in the summer.'

'My, that sounds perfect!' Lavender smiled. 'It was my father who named me after the sea lavender growing in the lighthouse garden. But, Bryony, dear . . .' Lavender shook her head. 'As I can't prove Father ever *owned* the place, I fear I must let my dreams go.'

'No!' cried Bryony. 'We must never let our

dreams go! We must find a way of making them happen!'

Lavender smiled, pausing by the garden gate.

'Lavender,' said Bryony, 'do you remember anything at all? Like who dealt with buying houses and stuff when you lived in the lighthouse?'

Just the smallest thing, Bryony felt sure, might lead to something useful. Ebony Swann never let anything go.

'No, I don't think,' Lavender began, 'that I can remember any—' She stopped.

'Yes?' Bryony prompted. 'Just say what's in your head! Quick – before it disappears!'

'Well, it might not mean anything . . .' Lavender went on, '. . . but I do remember a man with a gold pocket watch. He came once when my father wanted to know who owned the field next door. I remember my cat Marmalade was a kitten then, and he snuck into the man's briefcase that day. The case – it was more like a travel bag actually, or one that a doctor might use – anyway, Marmalade left a *puddle* in there, you know?'

Bryony nodded. 'And what happened next?'

'Well, no one saw, but I was rather scared,'

continued Lavender, 'and set about trying to mop up the wee while Father and the man with the pocket watch talked. Oh, and his briefcase – I have a vague memory it had the man's initials on the front. Yes – three! I remember trying to guess what he might be called.'

'What were they?' asked Bryony. 'Think really hard!'

Lavender peered up into the dark night sky like she was searching them out in the stars . . .

'W A . . . P? No – B!' cried Lavender. 'W A B – that's what they were! But that's all I can remember, I'm afraid. E-except the smell, but that was simply kitten wee!'

Lavender smiled and Bryony smiled too.

'Make your dreams happen too,' said Lavender. She walked through the gate and turned to Bryony. 'Don't give up hope about the gymkhana, eh?'

Bryony nodded back, thinking about this. Maybe Lavender was right. She had never been a quitter before, so why start now? She just needed to find the courage to see Abi tomorrow and ask if there was anything that could be done.

Bryony told Lavender they must meet again

before Lavender left on Monday. Waving her off down the starry lane, Bryony's head was heavy with thoughts.

'W A B . . .' she said slowly to herself. 'Hmm . . .'

Back inside, Bryony burst into her bedroom where Emma was tucked up in her sleeping bag.

'Em!' cried Bryony. 'Lavender's just remembered what might be a vital lighthouse clue.'

'What?' gasped Emma, sitting up at once, and Bryony quickly told her about the man with the briefcase. They just had to crack who W A B was and then they could get Lavender back in the lighthouse where she belonged!

'So where could the old deeds be?' wondered Bryony. 'W A B . . . ? W A B?' She repeated the initials. 'I wonder what they stand for,' she said. 'And although that man isn't likely to be around *now*, maybe he still has relatives here?

'It's a long shot, I know,' Bryony said. 'But any leads are better than none. Hey, hang on – I've just had an idea!'

She dashed downstairs and when she reappeared she was carrying an ancient phone book. The old owners had left it along with lists of things like bin collection days, mobile library van visits and the name of the man who swept the chimney.

'This might help you remember some old families,' said Bryony, 'whose relatives are still about!' She opened the heavy tome and flicked to the 'B's.

'Bry, how many of them *are* there?' Emma asked.

'Not that many!' replied Bryony quickly. 'Maybe . . . a couple of thousand? That's all. Right then – A. Bat, looks like he's the first one! How long have the Bats been around here, Em?'

'Um . . .' Emma scratched her head. 'So, I know there are Bumbles in Seahorse Lane, but I've never heard of any Bats. There's the Betts – and I *think* we have a Bitby, or Botby – are you sure it's Bat, not Batsby?'

'I'm sure,' replied Bryony. 'See, it says here – A. Bat.'

As Emma wracked her brains, Bryony considered trying a spot of tightrope-walking as that was what Ebony Swann did when trying to solve a tricky case. The problem was, she couldn't find her skipping rope so she tried a few handstands instead.

'What?' shrugged Bryony, already out of puff as Emma watched, looking puzzled.

'It'll help me think,' said Bryony. 'Really. You'll see.'

But secretly she hoped they'd find the right 'B' really soon because handstanding all night was going to be tough. No wonder, thought Bryony, that Ebony Swann just walked. Wobbling (occasionally) was *nothing* compared to a whole night of upside-down-ness!

Chapter 10

'Whoa – slow down!' Abi cried as Bryony burst into the Seaview Stables tack room with her brother and all of her friends.

She had fallen asleep on the phone book late last night around the Boggis-Wilsons, Emma having dozed off on the Bensons much earlier.

Today, though, having no further leads on the man with the pocket watch wasn't Bryony's main concern. She'd woken early with the gymkhana at the front of her mind, telling Emma and Josh she was going to ask Abi if she could – somehow – get her back in the gymkhana. Josh had felt Abi was more likely to reconsider if Bryony took 'backup' with her, so he'd shot off on his bike to round up the rest of the gang.

Bryony plonked down a huge tangle of bunting, carefully folded by her mum late last night and now totally messed up by the breezy sprint over.

'But, Abi!' puffed Bryony, very out of breath. 'Please can I ride Red in the gymkhana tomorrow? I know I sometimes act all grown up like everything's totally fine – but actually I've been waiting my entire life to have a pony of my own. And Red really is the most perfect pony that I could *ever* hope to have – and . . .'

As Bryony paused to draw breath, Abi raised a hand. Bryony glanced at the others, who all looked as determined as she did . . .

Josh was on the end, with his Team Coach cap on and his clipboard and stopwatch ready for practice. Next to him was Alice, rosy-cheeked and usually smiley – though she appeared much more serious today. Then there was Finn, with a Pony Club Gymkhana rule book under his arm (which he probably knew every word of!). Tapping her foot next to Finn was straight-talking Hari, who, Bryony saw, was glaring at Abi with a face like thunder. Finally, there was quiet, gentle Emma with her arm around Bryony's shoulder. Bryony felt so lucky to have such great friends.

'Okay, guys,' Abi said. 'There's no need to go on. I've already made up my mind. I had Bryony's *other* fan club here earlier too.'

Bryony looked puzzled. 'My other fan club?' she asked, and Abi went on to explain.

'First your grandpa,' said Abi. 'Then your friend, Lavender. They both came offering to help me type up a new programme, and even deliver them to the stables in Cockledore and Nettleton, if I can find Sara a different pony so that you can have Red.'

Bryony blushed, suddenly feeling all this fuss on her behalf made her sound a little bit spoiled. And spoiled was the last thing she ever wanted to be.

'S-sorry,' mumbled Bryony quietly, looking down at her feet awkwardly.

'No, don't be,' Abi replied. 'Bryony, listen, your grandpa and Lavender are both right. And you were right to come here and speak up too. It was actually very brave of you, and kind of all your friends too. The fact is, you *do* deserve to ride

Red on Saturday after all the hard work you, and he, have put in since the summer. I had already decided that overnight so—'

'So I can *ride* him?' Bryony cut in. Her sea-green eyes were suddenly wide and her windblown hair, usually unruly, today was a total mess!

'I'm actually back in the gymkhana?' asked Bryony. 'Just – just me on Red?'

'Just you,' Abi nodded. 'The mix-up wasn't your fault. But I still need to find another pony for Sara Wells . . .'

'Piggy!' beamed Emma suddenly. 'Sara can share Piggy with me! Why didn't I think of that before? It would be great for me to watch a better rider than *me* on him and it might help Piggy learn new things too.'

'Are you sure that's okay, Emma?' Abi asked.

'Really, Em?' Bryony said.

'Yes, I'm totally sure,' smiled Emma. 'If Sara doesn't *mind* being on Piggy, that is? I mean, he isn't the *fastest* pony in the world. But he generally gets there in the end.'

Abi nodded. 'I actually think Piggy might be better for Sara than Red as Piggy's a bit more . . .'

'Of a nightmare?' said Emma.

'Challenging,' grinned Abi. 'Let's just say *challenging*, yes?'

Bryony could hardly believe it. She was back in the gymkhana! Now she could show Red off to everyone!

Abi turned to Bryony. 'Right,' she said. 'I'll let your grandpa and Lavender know that the programme is ready to be changed.'

'O-or I could let them know!' Bryony beamed eagerly. 'I could even nip round to Gramps on Red now, i-if you have the programme layout on a data stick?'

'I'll get it,' smiled Abi, heading out as Bryony's friends all gathered round her.

'Never mind The Fabulous Five,' laughed Josh. 'The Super Six ride again!'

'Six?' huffed Hari. 'There are *five* of us, Coach.'

'No, six,' insisted Josh. ''Cos I'm on my bike. And that's riding *without* the pongy mucking out! Which is what *I* call *sensible*.'

'Hey, I don't mind the mucking out!' beamed Bryony. She didn't mind anything today! She was already thinking of what she wanted to practise with Red ahead of the gymkhana tomorrow. She couldn't wait to tell Red the great news. He was going to be over the moon!

*

The rest of the morning went like a dream. Red had a twinkle in his eyes, and a spring in his step, and later on at the beach, as the children put the ponies through their paces, Red didn't put a hoof out of place, despite the gusty wind.

'Well done!' praised Bryony, patting his side. 'You're amazing!'

As well as all the usual events, Bryony's group had been picked to do a musical pony dance tomorrow. It wasn't to be judged. It was just meant to be an entertaining thing to watch during the afternoon tea break.

The friends had practised this dance a lot. It was going to be performed to the *Pirates of the Caribbean* music. Hari had come up with the idea, because that music was really exciting, she said. And of course they lived by the sea.

The ponies were meant to be the pirates but the children riding them would wear the pirate costumes. They'd also wave pirate cutlasses, which would be plastic, although at first Hari had wanted the real thing. Finn, however, had done some research and, although the Pony Club Rule Book had no mention whatsoever of pirate accessories, he thought, on balance, that real swords would probably not be allowed. Plus, the kiosk on the seafront only sold toy ones.

Josh and Bryony had been allowed to borrow their mum's phone with the music on for everyone to practise. Tomorrow, however, Abi had said that they'd have a proper sound system.

Bryony felt so excited as Josh set the music playing and everyone went through the dance for one final time. As she took Red through his moves, Bryony thought Hari was right. With its turquoise sea and craggy white cliffs like the torn ragged lace on their pirate shirts, there was no place better on earth to do this dance than in Brook Dale!

Red's head was high as he trotted along the golden sand. Bryony could see he was really listening as well, with one ear forward and the other back, as she led him smoothly through his moves. First, the ponies had to walk around in a circle, like pirates having a chat – or 'parley' was the proper word, Finn had informed them. He had at least twenty books on pirates at home!

The pony parley was meant to decide how they'd split the treasure the pirate ponies had just stolen. Tomorrow the audience would see a large open treasure chest, and this would be overflowing with treasure.

But the pirates could not agree who would have what. So the next part of the dance would see them splitting apart to prepare to fight each other for the treasure. They would trot forward in two lines of two, one behind the other – except for Piggy, who would now head away in the opposite direction and wait in the wings for his 'big moment' later on.

When the front pony heading up each pair came in line with the treasure chest, they would turn (each line going the opposite way to the other) and sweep back down the way they'd just come, and this would be repeated twice.

Now it was time for the fight to begin! Each pony pair would move into a side-by-side position and do a series of weaving crossovers with the other pony pair as the pirates showed off to each other, trying to put off their opponents! Tornado and Red were pirate partners and so were Princess P and Daffy. At this point Piggy was still waiting motionless at the side for his cue. Piggy, thought Bryony, was superb at this 'waiting motionless' bit!

Then for the finale! When the music reached a daring pirate-y crescendo, Piggy – who was meant to be Captain Jack Sparrow – had to trot on as feistily as he could with Emma waving a pirate flag wildly.

The other pirate ponies, upon seeing the fiercely determined glint in Captain Piggy Sparrow's eyes, would scatter in all directions leaving the way clear for Piggy to head straight for the treasure chest!

This treasure chest was really a cardboard box. But Emma and her little brother, Will, had done the most fantastic painting job on it, so now it looked very authentic. For the run-through today, the chest was empty – but tomorrow they'd fill it up with treasure! The treasure was lots of jewellery (cheap but incredibly sparkly!)

that Bryony had bought from a charity shop in Nettleton last week.

Captain Piggy Sparrow, upon tearing up and reaching the treasure chest, would then circle it triumphantly, indicating he was the winner. The crowd would burst into rapturous applause and Miss Pigeon would, no doubt, announce that she absolutely *knew* that that would happen. '*Go Piggy Sparrow!*' the crowd would shout. '*Hooray!*'

Earlier in the week, their practice sessions had been dodgy, to say the least. It was difficult getting Piggy to move at the right time, or at all. At one point Emma had suggested that she and Piggy should be pulled from the routine. But Hari had pointed out that they needed an odd number and so Piggy just had to do his best.

Today, however, as the final bar of music faded, Piggy – to everyone's amazement and delight – circled the treasure chest like a little pirate pro! And even Hari punched the air triumphantly . . .

'Whoo-hoo!'

Afterwards, they gathered in the shade of caves to let the ponies cool off while they had a 'debrief talk' from Josh.

'That was the best Piggy has ever done!' he said.

'Yeah, he was wonderful, Em!' beamed Bryony.

'What have you *done* to him?' giggled Alice.

'Dunno,' shrugged Emma. 'Maybe he just rides better if he thinks he's a pirate?'

'Well, it *is* interesting . . .' Finn began, 'how ponies – and people too, research has shown – tend to take on the persona that's *expected* of them. I was once reading a book where this eminent equine behaviourist—'

'Whoa, Finn, maybe later, yeah?' Hari cut in before Finn embarked on a long lecture filled with facts that no one understood.

'I say,' concluded Hari, 'that from now on, guys, we just call Piggy "Piggy *Sparrow*" and that should do it?'

Everyone nodded their agreement.

'Piggy Sparrow it is, then!' Emma said proudly.

'Right, then,' said Josh, 'that's about it. You've all been so good today, I don't have anything else to say – apart from do everything like that tomorrow and it'll be cool!'

As they set off back to Seaview, everyone was in such a good mood. Everything was starting to come together. Red led the way back along the prom, and as they went Bryony glimpsed the old lighthouse in the distance on the cliffs. She thought of Lavender and how kind she'd been with the bunting and then to show up and help her this morning. It was Bryony's turn to help Lavender make her dreams come true now too. She just had to get to the bottom of the W A B clue!

Emma had agreed to give Sara a go on Piggy Sparrow during the lunch break.

'I think she's going to like him,' Alice said, ever the enthusiast.

'Especially if he keeps up the good work,' added Hari. 'And I shall be watching my Miss Daffodil like a hawk tomorrow. Won't I, young lady?' Hari said as Daffodil's right ear bent towards her. Then cheeky little Daffy let out a snort that sounded distinctly like a raspberry!

'And the same to you!' Hari replied with a laugh.

Bryony loved the way the spring sunshine was bringing out the warm toffee-apple-coloured tones in Red's glossy coat as they walked uphill to the stables.

'Pony pamper time this afternoon,' she said

to Alice. The ponies were going to have the full treatment to get them and their kit spick and span for tomorrow.

'Hooray!' Alice cheered. 'I can't wait! I finally get to braid Princess's mane!'

Bryony thought of Georgina's palomino. Beau never had a hair out of place. That wasn't normal, she decided. Red wouldn't be kept *always* so prim and proper that he was never allowed a second of fun!

She briefly wondered if Georgina had yet found out that Bryony and Red were back in the gymkhana *together* despite her best efforts to part them. The sooner she accepted that Bryony and Red were a team the better.

'Oh, Red,' beamed Bryony, patting his neck, 'I do love you so much!' She breathed in his beautiful cinnamon smell.

Red gave a little snort. It sounded soft and low and tender. The kind he saved for special moments – like when she first opened his stable door in the morning, and before she left him every night.

'I know, you love me too,' whispered Bryony.

'And tomorrow we are going to show *everyone* just how brilliant you are!'

*

That afternoon Seaview Stables buzzed with the excited air of a rapidly approaching gymkhana.

People bustled about looking for this or that – the right dandy brush, some saddle soap and tack care sponge. The last of which no one could *ever* seem to find when they really needed one, like today!

'And make sure you wring it out until *almost dry* before applying the saddle soap,' Tabby's mum was telling anyone who'd listen. 'We'll show Cockledore and Nettleton how to sparkle!'

There were also children who had grown considerably since the last gymkhana and needed to swap hacking jackets. Others, entering the dressage events, were fine for elastic bands but some were on needle hunts for sewing the braided mane into bobbles. Usually Alice was the one to go to for all things dressage!

One glove or one riding boot were also very typical things that unhelpfully went missing the day before a gymkhana. And hoof oil!

'Anyone got hoof oil?' called a boy, marching past the open stable doors.

'Try Tabby!' shouted someone. 'She's got *everything.*'

'I have some too!' Bryony announced and a host of children raced to Red's stable door shouting . . .

'Me first!'

When Red's tack and Bryony's riding boots were positively gleaming, she turned her attention to Red himself. Seaview Stables, being a relatively small riding school, did not have individual turnout paddocks for each pony so, slinging her carry bag of grooming equipment over her shoulder, Bryony took Red outside to the large group turnout paddock, which was heaving with ponies.

Bryony actually preferred this to the individual paddocks that her old city riding school had, because when ponies were all together like this, it was far more sociable. Besides, Red seemed to like the company.

Jess, one of the older girls, who had looked out for Bryony since she'd joined Seaview, had just finished grooming her pony – a glossy chestnut called Destiny.

'Here, Bry, you can have my spot,' called Jess, walking Destiny over with a smile.

'Ooh, she looks so shiny!' said Bryony.

'And so she should,' Jess laughed. 'I've been at it for ages. Anyway, it's worth it. Or I hope it will be tomorrow. Hey, Bry, Camilla said you and Red weren't competing together.'

'No – that was just a mix-up,' replied Bryony brightly as Red and Destiny gave each other a friendly little nuzzle.

'Did Georgina Brook happen to have anything to do that "mix-up"?' asked Jess. She knew what Georgina was like.

'Well, actually,' Bryony nodded, 'yes, she did.'

'Watch her tomorrow, Bry,' warned Jess. 'Like, I know we should all be grateful because the gymkhana's in their beautiful fields, but Georgina doesn't care if Brook Dale takes the Golden Horseshoe as long as she comes out top in her own events. She was definitely like that last year on Flint, the pony she had before Red.'

Bryony nodded.

'And,' added Jess, 'Georgina would do *anything* to win, if you get my drift?'

'Yes, I do,' Bryony replied. She was all too familiar with Georgina's underhand tricks and schemes. 'Thanks, Jess,' said Bryony. 'I'll watch out for her.'

'Good.'

Jess said she'd better be off because she still had lots to do. Patting Destiny's gleaming coat, she walked her pony on. 'Good luck for tomorrow, by the way,' Jess called.

'Thanks! You too,' Bryony smiled, leading Red over to Destiny's space and tying him to the paddock fence. Two ponies along was Emma's Piggy, and Emma seemed to be having trouble getting the curry comb through his thick Shetland coat.

'You okay, Em?' Bryony called along.

'Not really!' Emma called back. 'So I washed Piggy down, but now he's dry his coat feels more matted than ever. Honestly, he looks like a small baby yak! I just can't get the comb through.'

'Like my hair in the morning!' Bryony joked. 'Hey, listen – do you want a hand, I could do Red later?'

'That's really kind,' called Emma, 'but take the

paddock space while you can get it. The place is so busy.'

'I know, but so exciting!' said Bryony. The time before a gymkhana always felt like the build-up to Christmas Day for her. The wait was always thrilling!

Red stood very well as Bryony got him ready to be bathed. First, shc picked out any bits in his hoofs, then curry-combed and dandy-brushed his coat to get out any mud. She also used a wide-toothed mane comb on his manc and tail.

'Oh, and we mustn't forget your little star,' she said, finally drawing the dandy brush over the small white star between Red's eyes. Red breathed out and his warm breath on the back of her hand made Bryony's heart melt. She closed her eyes, wanting to remember this moment for ever.

Now that Red was thoroughly brushed out, she took him over to the area set aside for bathing the ponies. She tied Red up with a quick-release knot, and then, soaking a sponge in warm water, she squeezed it out and washed Red's face following the direction of his hair and making sure she didn't get any water in his eyes.

'Well done,' said Bryony, as Red stood nice and still for her.

Next, Bryony hosed his coat all over. Some ponies didn't like the hose but Red had always been fine with it. She started with his hooves and worked upwards, allowing Red to get used to what she was doing.

When he was wet all over, she shampooed him using a sponge, being careful not to use too much and avoiding his face altogether. Bryony made sure she gave him a good rinse down, removing every single trace of foamy bubbles.

It was time to dry Red now. Bryony used a sweat scraper, drawing it along his coat to get off as much water as she could. Then, talking to him about tomorrow, she rubbed him down with a soft chamois cloth and rinsed his tail before taking him for a quick ten-minute walk to let the sunshine him off completely.

When Red was dry, Bryony used her fingers to undo any knots in his mane, before combing it through gently. 'Now it's time to go and visit Alice!' she said.

Both Red and Princess Perla needed their manes

braided for the dressage event tomorrow. Alice showed Bryony what to do on Princess P first and then Bryony copied on Red.

'That's it,' said Alice. Bryony was really gentle and was trying to be as neat as she could. If only she was this careful with her own hair, she thought, it might *occasionally* look half decent!

By the time they had finished, both ponies looked amazing. Their braids were perfect, their tails nice and full, and, after a quick dandy-brush all over, their freshly-washed coats came up a treat too.

'How very smart you are, Red!' said Bryony and Red gave a whinny of delight.

But he was starting to look sleepy too. As she'd finished off the braiding, Bryony had noticed that Red's eyes had been half-closed and his ears had flopped to the side. One of his back legs had also been raised, a sure sign he was ready for a nap. Sweet Red, thought Bryony. All this serious pampering must have exhausted him!

Thanking Alice for her help, Bryony took Red back to his stable, where she left him to have a doze.

'I'll see you later,' Bryony whispered. 'Smart boy.'

It was still very busy outside and fast approaching three o'clock. Bryony wondered how Emma was getting on with Piggy's outrageously wild coat and she found them still out in the paddock.

'Need a hand, Em?' Bryony asked.

'Yes, please,' replied Emma, clearly flagging.

As Bryony helped her finish off, who should stride past but Georgina Brook, probably on her way to see her relay team.

'Sara seeing to Red, is she?' Georgina asked Bryony, looking very smug indeed. Clearly she hadn't heard that Bryony was back in the gymkhana.

'Actually,' Bryony answered, 'Red's all done, and he looks amazing. And for your information, he was groomed by his rider, *me*.'

Georgina's eyes narrowed. 'You ... *you're* riding him?'

'That's right!' Bryony nodded. 'Your unfortunate "mix-up" has all been sorted out.'

Georgina looked livid. Her pale cheeks flashed magenta and her eyes could have frozen you solid.

'Well, don't go thinking,' Georgina hissed, 'he stands a *chance* of beating my Beau. Especially in the show jumping. Beau is faultless, you'll see.'

'I guess I will,' Bryony replied. 'And so will everyone else. They'll see for themselves if Red is "useless" like you've always said he is. Or not.'

Georgina smiled and raised a white-blonde eyebrow. Bryony could just make out a hint of nervousness in her eyes. Bryony herself was nervous too, after what Jess had said earlier.

As Georgina flicked back her shiny blonde hair and marched off, her nose in the air, Bryony couldn't help but feel that Jess was right. If there was a way to embarrass Red and Bryony tomorrow, Georgina wouldn't rest until she'd found it!

Chapter 11

While Red had a well-deserved nap, Bryony hurried away to find Grandpa and Lavender. She wanted to say thank you for not only redoing, but also redelivering, all the gymkhana programmes.

Bryony called at Grandpa's first but he wasn't home, so she decided to head to The Ticklish Trout, Lavender's B&B, to hopefully catch her there.

It was nice and sunny as Bryony made her way there through the town's main street. The crooked houses always made her smile. It looked like they had crash-landed from the sky and no one had thought to straighten them! Bryony loved their old timber frames and small casement windows made up of thick squares of glass. Sometimes the glass had the odd little bubble. These, she considered, must once have been floating, but had set as the molten glass cooled and went solid. A bubble in time – seen by generations, and now her!

Here and there, perched on the windowsills, were neat wooden boxes jam-packed with flowers: small lilac crocuses, pale yellow primulas and an occasional bold red tulip – which seemed to shout as it towered above the rest: 'Hey! Not them! Look at me!'

As she skipped along brushing the flowery confetti, Bryony suddenly spotted Lavender talking to Grandpa just outside the post office. Beside them was a large blue flowerpot crammed with custard-coloured daffodils. Touch *them*, thought Bryony, and Miss Pigeon would be out in a shot!

'Hi!' Bryony waved, running over.

'Hello, Pumpkin,' said Grandpa.

'Oh, Bryony!' beamed Lavender. 'Have you had a lovely day?'

'Yes, thanks to you two!' Bryony replied. 'Thanks so much for everything you've done. But, Gramps, how did you get the new programmes out to Cockledore and Nettleton?' Bryony remembered Grandpa had sold his car last year.

'I borrowed your mum's car,' Grandpa smiled. 'We even found a tin of mints in it and polished most of them off! I was just going to buy some more in the post office now before it shuts.'

'Good idea,' smiled Lavender. 'It was so lovely visiting Nettleton again, Bryony. I used to go there occasionally when I was young, to the theatre to see a show at Christmas time. It's been quite a day for catching up. I saw Eliza Pigeon for coffee this morning too, and I've just been to tea with Dorothea Parsley.'

'*Huh! Excuse me!*' said a sudden voice. Miss Pigeon had come out of the post office to water the pot of daffodils on the step. 'Did my ears just hear right, Lavender Moon? You've just been to tea with that warty old TOAD?!'

'Lavender *Moon* . . .' Bryony repeated under her breath. 'Moon' must have been Lavender's maiden name, she thought, when she lived here as a girl. She tucked this fact away in her brain like Ebony Swann often did, in case it came in useful later on.

Grandpa swiftly left (without his mints for Mum!) and as Lavender went to answer a fuming Miss Pigeon, Miss Pigeon started ranting again . . .

'Parsley never invited *me* to tea!' she scowled. 'Not that I care a fig! And I hope you didn't eat any of her jam – as mine's better an' everyone knows it! An' if her cottage is as full of rubbish as her shed is I'm surprised you had anywhere to sit! I've seen that shed over me garden wall. Full of clutter!'

It now struck Bryony that, as the two Miss Ps had been around as long as Lavender, Miss Pigeon might remember the person who'd dealt with property all those years ago. After all, she had a memory like an elephant!

'Miss Pigeon,' said Bryony, 'when you were young, who dealt with selling houses, and other buildings, around here? Do you remember?' Any help to narrow down the rest of the 'B's in the phone book would be great!

'It was 'im at the Big House!' Miss Pigeon replied at once. 'That relative of them Brooks that live there now. And it wasn't just—'

'Yoo-hoo!' Another familiar voice drowned her

out, and up bustled a red-faced Miss Parsley. ''Ere, Lavender,' she said, holding out a lilac scarf. 'You left your scarf at the cottage earlier so—'

'I'm surprised she could find *space* for it!' Miss Pigeon cut in. 'And kindly stop INTERRUPTING private conversations! I was saying summat when you WOBBLED UP!'

'NO NEED TO SHOUT!' boomed Miss Parsley back. 'You old GOAT!'

As the two Miss Ps argued on, and Lavender watched, trying not to grin, Bryony was thinking about what Miss Pigeon had said before Miss Parsley had arrived.

Miss Pigeon had just revealed that the person who dealt with property sales when Lavender was a girl was a relative of the current Brooks! Then Bryony recalled that Lavender, only yesterday, had said she thought that Georgina's great-grandfather, Algernon Brook, might have been a *lawyer.*

Of course! thought Bryony – lawyers *did* deal with property. Hadn't she, herself, assumed last night at supper that Georgina's lawyer dad was the one handling the current lighthouse sale? So perhaps his ancestor, Algernon, had handled the *original* sale to Lavender's father? Maybe *he* was the one who had come to see Lavender's dad with the briefcase and gold pocket watch? Algernon Brook! Yes! Why not?

So if Algernon Brook, she thought, once had the deeds proving that the lighthouse *did* belong to Lavender's dad – and so now to Lavender – Bryony just had to find those deeds and Lavender could stay!

But where to start looking? Well, Georgina's house was the obvious place! People did keep their relatives' things if they inherited their estate and house sometimes. *Especially* if those things might be useful to them, and paperwork and books on law stuff might well, she thought, be useful to children, or *grandchildren* – like Austin Brook, who followed in the family footsteps to become a lawyer too!

If Algernon's briefcase was still in the Manor, then maybe – just *maybe* – the lighthouse deeds might still be inside it. Or if not, they might be among piles of old paperwork somewhere very close to it?

Bryony knew this was a long shot, but it was

all she had right now. Lavender would be leaving on Monday so Bryony had to act fast. She would search the house – on Saturday – when she'd be in the grounds of Brook Dale for the gymkhana. 'Yes!' she gasped to herself. Being there anyway gave her the perfect opportunity!

So where to start looking? It had to be the attic! She wouldn't tell Lavender what she was planning, as the last thing she wanted was to build her hopes up, only to find nothing. She *would* tell Emma though, she thought. But not until after the gymkhana, as Emma had enough to think about right now.

Bryony's tummy was turning somersaults. Not only was she beyond excited about the upcoming gymkhana, but she might also unearth the very thing to allow Lavender to stay in Brook Dale for good! The sooner tomorrow came the better!

'Lavender, I'd love you to watch me in the gymkhana tomorrow,' said Bryony over the noise of the squabbling Miss Ps.

'What?' cried Miss Pigeon, ears like a bat. 'I'd like to come and watch you too!'

'So would I!' snorted Miss Parsley.

'Great!' cried Bryony. Red would have his own little fan club.

'I was also wondering . . .' Bryony turned now to Miss Pigeon, 'as you're so . . . brilliant at reading the future, if you might be able to give me an idea if me and Red might do okay?'

Miss Pigeon positively beamed at this. 'I'd be delighted to!' she said, flouncing up the shop's step. 'Come on then, what are you waiting for, girly?'

'Blooming fortune-telling,' muttered Miss Parsley with a tut. 'Load of rubbish if you ask me.'

'Well, no one IS asking you!' replied Miss Pigeon. 'So there!'

Lavender nodded at Bryony. 'See you tomorrow,' she smiled.

'Yes, and I will too!' Miss Parsley added with a sniff.

Nodding, Bryony waved and followed Miss Pigeon inside.

The post office was empty as it was the end of the day. Miss Pigeon bustled behind the counter, and, taking a stick of liquorice from one of the sweet jars, she handed it to Bryony.

'Suck on this while I put the kettle on,' she winked. 'Won't be long.'

Bryony wasn't sure what exactly was going on but thanked her for the free sweet. Grinning, Miss P disappeared through an old pine door into the shop's back room and came back five minutes later with a cup of tea – and also now dressed in her fortune-telling costume, the same one she wore at various fêtes.

Bryony had to force down a grin. Miss Pigeon looked so funny dressed as Mademoiselle Oiseau, with her curly black wig, big hooped earrings and wrist full of jangly bracelets.

Miss Pigeon – or Mademoiselle Oiseau – passed the tea to Bryony, who was now sitting on an old stool by the counter.

'Blow on it to cool it first!' Miss P instructed. 'Then drink it up, leaving a little bit of tea at the bottom, mind you.'

Bryony nodded, now realising Miss Pigeon was about to read her tea leaves to see how she and Red would do on Saturday. She had read Bryony's tea leaves once before and it had not ended well.

Bryony did as she was told, drinking down the tea and making sure to leave a little at the bottom.

'That's the way!' smiled Miss Pigeon, her violet eyes twinkling. She whipped a stick of liquorice from behind her left ear and sucked on it enthusiastically, as if that would help to clear her mystical airways. 'Well!' she snapped. 'What you waiting for? Pass the cup over then, girly! I ain't got all week!'

Bryony handed it to her at once and Miss Pigeon peered in. One more suck on the liquorice stick and bingo! – tomorrow's mystical visions were *tumbling* out . . .

'I see a field, I see a pony, and another . . . and another!'

'That might be because it's a gymkhana?' offered Bryony, trying not to sound overly smart.

'Huh! I KNOWS that!' Miss Pigeon puffed. 'Oh, wait! I sees summat *else* . . . gold.'

'*Gold?*' gasped Bryony. That sounded much more promising!

'A golden rosette?' suggested Bryony. 'With "First Place!" on it maybe? O-or perhaps a Golden Horseshoe trophy?'

'No, 'tis more like *sticky* gold,' Miss Pigeon went on. 'And 'appen it's nutty as well.'

'Oh.' Bryony's face suddenly fell. She felt very puzzled too. 'A sticky, nutty kind of gold?' she said. 'I wonder what *that* could be?'

But suddenly Mademoiselle Oiseau announced that her mystical radar was getting 'all foggy' and she couldn't possibly make another single prediction now. Not one.

Bryony wondered if it had something to do with the fact that it was precisely five o'clock and at this time Saul Salmon did a deal called 'Half Price Fish at Five on Friday Night'! But anyway, thought Bryony, it was time for her to be getting back to Red too.

'Oh, all right, well thank you, Miss Pigeon – I mean – Mademoiselle Oiseau,' she said.

'Aye,' replied the old lady, grabbing a packet of salt and a bottle of vinegar off the shelf and hurrying to get her coat off the hat stand. 'Oh, and mind you stay away from golden sticky nutty things at that gymkhana tomorrow now, won't you!'

'I . . . yeah,' Bryony nodded back, having *no* idea what she was on about. 'Thanks,' she smiled. 'Good plan. I'll certainly, um . . . try.'

Stepping out with a wave, she rushed back to Red to muck him out and feed him. She wanted to make sure she had plenty of time to talk to him about the gymkhana too. She needed to tell him that, whatever happened, she was so very proud of him. Tomorrow was such a big day, and Bryony was totally ready!

Chapter 12

'Wow!' gasped Bryony as she sat on Red, looking around at the busy, happy scene.

It was a little after nine in the morning and everyone was gathering at Brook Dale Manor for The 80th Three Coves Gymkhana. How brilliant to be here after all the build-up, thought Bryony.

She had to pinch herself to prove that this was really happening. Not only was she going to ride her *very own* pony in a gymkhana, but that pony was the one of her dreams . . .

Bryony gazed down at Red's braids. The sun was shining and drawing out the beautiful toffee-apple shades in his coat too. Bryony patted his neck and Red breathed out softly. Already she felt so proud to be showing him off!

'Oh, Red,' whispered Bryony. 'We're going to have the *best* day ever!'

She turned to Emma, who was sitting on an unusually tidy Piggy. Bryony and Emma had just walked through the Manor's gardens from Emma's little cottage by thc back gate. And the place looked ever so beautiful today – from the velvety lawns, to the frilly flowers, and of course all their bunting! It was draped from tree to tree and fluttered in the breeze, all the little coloured flags so neat and bright – and so *many* of them too. Their bunting was everywhere!

'How are you feeling, Em?' Bryony asked, suddenly sensing she was rather quiet.

'Really nervous, to be honest,' replied Emma.

'Nerves aren't always a bad thing,' said Bryony. 'Try not to worry too much though, or Piggy will pick up on your nerves.'

'I'll try my best.' Emma nodded. 'And thanks for all your help, Bry.'

'No worries.'

Bryony was desperate to tell Emma about her

secret mission to search Georgina's attic later on but Emma seemed so on edge right now, and was so distracted by Piggy, that Bryony thought it best to just let her get through the day first, then tell her.

Bryony looked down the Manor's sweeping driveway to the lane just outside, which was fast filling up with freshly-washed horseboxes and trailers. Bordering the lane, over a neat hedge, was one of the Brooks' many fields. Here stalls selling gifts, clothes and food were being set up so as not to damage the Manor's pristine lawns. Raised seating was also being put up so that supporters from all three towns could sit and watch all the light-hearted, fun games scheduled to take place there.

'Let's go down and watch by the gate,' said Bryony.

'O-okay,' replied Emma. She swallowed hard. 'Time to see how Piggy reacts to a crowd.'

'He'll be fine.'

They walked their ponies down the front drive and out of the large iron gates. Bryony adored all the early-morning hustle and bustle just before a gymkhana. She could see that Red was excited too as he watched, with fluffy pricked-up ears, a flurry of ponies arriving. There were Welsh Cobs and cute little Shetlands, and palominos, and New Forest ponies and some bays (though none, thought Bryony, were anywhere *near* as lovely as her Red!).

She paused for a moment as she wanted all this to seep into her memory for ever. Ponies were whinnying, and excited riders talking tactics, all in their very best riding clothes.

The girls then followed a group of riders from Peak Point into the huge Fun Games field.

'So far so good, Piggy,' Emma said as Piggy, though slow, walked nicely beside Red. Bryony loved how Red showed Piggy what to do. It was almost like he thought of himself as Piggy's big brother!

'Oh, more bunting!' Bryony giggled, looking around this huge field. The spectators' raised seating was so covered in it, that it looked as if the Queen might be coming. Bryony figured she'd be dreaming about bunting for weeks!

'Bry, there are the others,' said Emma, pointing, and Bryony saw the rest of the gang arrive along with Josh, who'd come on his bike.

'Yay!' cheered Bryony. 'Let's go over and see them.'

They trotted across and the ponies greeted each other with friendly little snorts and nuzzles.

'Oh, everyone looks so smart!' smiled Bryony. 'And whatever happens we're a team, and all proud of each other, right?'

'You said it!' beamed Josh. 'The Super Six forever!'

'How's Red today, Bry?' Josh patted his side.

'In really good form!' Bryony replied. He felt relaxed and was taking all the clattering trailers completely in his stride.

'How's Tornado, Finn?' Bryony asked.

'So far so good,' Finn replied. 'Fingers crossed.'

'Look – Cockledore and Nettleton are arriving too!' gasped Alice. Bryony followed her glance to the parking field next door, rapidly filling up with carloads of children Bryony had never seen before.

'Ooooo, I'm so excited I think I could burst!' giggled Alice. Her rosy cheeks were even pinker today and Princess Perla looked positively perfect.

'Please try not to burst,' grinned Hari. 'It would make so much mess. We want to keep the ponies looking their best!'

Everyone laughed. And Bryony got that wonderful frilly feeling of butterflies in her tummy. There was nothing quite like the excitement of gymkhana day – except maybe pony camp – and that was something *else* she had to look forward to!

'Seriously though, Alice,' Hari said, 'remember to try and stay calm.' Hari patted Daffodil's dapple grey neck and the little Welsh Connemara cross gave a very excited little blow. 'And *you* stay calm too, Miss Daffy,' Hari added. 'And *please* remember what we've learned!'

'Nice and tight round the turns,' Bryony nodded, starting to go through things in *her* head now too, like just before a test at school!

'No tugging on the reins, though,' added Finn.

'*Forget* the opposition!' Alice said with a grin. 'And clear commands – and stay focused!'

Everyone looked at Emma in case she wanted to add something.

'Um, remember to call Piggy – Piggy *Sparrow*,'

she gulped. 'Because that will make him, well, at least *move*. Oh! But what if I let you all down?'

'Oh, Em!' cried everyone cheerfully. 'You won't!'

Emma still looked mildly terrified, but Piggy didn't seem as if he could care less. For him, life was just one sweet series of yummy grass, broken up by dreamy dozes in the sunshine!

He'd never looked smarter than he did today though. Piggy's thick Shetland hair had been freshly brushed again that morning so for once you could actually see his sweet brown eyes!

In fact all the Seaview Stables' riders looked super-smart, thought Bryony. Brook Dale clearly took gymkhanas very seriously. And so, it appeared, did the other two riding schools, for the Cockledore and Nettleton riders also looked impeccable.

Bryony found herself remembering Park Lodge Stables, her old riding school in the city. It might have been because she was younger then, but gymkhanas there had seemed a little more relaxed. Park Lodge was bigger for one thing, with enough children to compete against each other and not have other stables come to visit.

But having visitors, like today, Bryony thought, brought out feelings of loyalty. It brought out a bit of rivalry too . . .

'What are the Seaview parents all wearing?' asked Bryony.

'Ah,' replied Hari. 'Well, the rumour was true. Tabby's mum *did* get all the Seaview parents matching green polo shirts with Seaview Stables on the back. Oh, and a photo of Tiberius and Tabby on the front, looking sweet – but very determined!'

'Oh!' Bryony burst out laughing. 'I don't believe it!'

Bryony was very relieved that all the riders had to wear more formal kit. She felt so good in her (nearly) new hacking jacket and cravat. And Red's tack and Bryony's riding boots were so shiny you could practically see your face in them. All the careful prep yesterday had certainly paid off!

'Has Mum got all the clothes for our pirate dance, Josh?' Bryony now asked.

'Yep,' replied Josh. 'And the treasure chest and all the swords and stuff.'

Bryony nodded. The treasure chest was now brim-full of shiny necklaces, bangles and long sparkly earrings. But as well as looking forward to the dance, there were so many games and great events coming up first!

'Look, Bry, there's Mum.' Josh pointed over his shoulder to the seating, now filling up with spectators. 'Can you see her?' he asked. 'Bottom row. Next to Emma's dad. They're the ones in the Tabby Tibby fan club polo shirts!'

'Yep, along with hundreds of others!' Bryony giggled.

Bryony suddenly picked her out and waved. She was so glad that Mum had made it in time after delivering all the beautiful wedding bouquets – very early – to the bride! But she should have known that her mum would be there. Mum wouldn't have missed this for the world!

Bryony and Emma headed over to say a quick hello before everything started. Grandpa and Lavender were also sitting beside Emma's dad.

'Hello!' Grandpa smiled.

'Lovely day for it!' said Lavender. She looked really excited to be there.

'Yes, perfect!' beamed Bryony, remembering her secret mission. She couldn't tell Lavender or she'd be bound to stop her. And even though it was a very long shot, Bryony was determined to try her best if it gave Lavender one final chance of being able to stay in Brook Dale for good.

'The ponies look so handsome!' said Lavender, lovingly patting Red.

'Even Piggy!' grinned Will. Emma's little brother loved having rides on Piggy when he was up at the farm with his sister, and today he'd come in his pony onesie saying it would give Emma and Bryony good luck!

'How are you feeling, girls?' asked Emma's dad.

'Nervous!' gulped Emma.

'Excited!' Bryony said. 'And nervous – and hopeful. I so want Red to look good in front of—'

She stopped, about to say Georgina Brook. But she mustn't let Georgina spoil her day. Like Alice had said, they just had to think about what *they* were doing. And have fun – lots and lots of it!

'I just want Red to have a lovely day,' Bryony said with a nod.

'I'm sure he will, and – oh, my!' said Lavender. 'Doesn't the bunting look beautiful?'

'Yes, and thanks for your help with it,' Bryony replied.

'My pleasure,' smiled Lavender. 'Everything looks a picture!'

As well as the stalls selling gifts and snacks, there were some with country clothes, tack and equipment. Bryony didn't know where to look first. It was like all the Christmas presents she'd ever wished for right before her eyes! Strings of pony fairy lights, and pony jumpers and pencil cases – it all looked so colourful and inviting! There was also an ice-cream van and even a stall offering pony-shaped candyfloss!

Some big silver vans were selling cooked food too. And right now it smelled like breakfast was on the go . . .

'Mmm, I think I smell sausages and bacon,' said Bryony.

'Piggy does too,' Emma groaned. 'Look at him!'

Piggy was sniffing wildly, his upper lip curled up to show a set of big teeth. They reminded Bryony of those funny sets of false ones you got in joke shops. The kind you wound up and they chattered.

'What's he *doing*?' gasped Emma. 'He's gone really weird.'

'No,' giggled Bryony. 'Ponies do that to smell better.'

Just then Georgina trotted by on Beau, looking down her nose at everyone. Beau looked majestic, and very powerful. Bryony thought Georgina must have been telling the truth when she'd said Beau jumped like a dream. Later Red would be competing against him in the Chase-me-Charlie, but as that was the last event of the day Bryony decided not to worry about it now.

Just then, a loudspeaker crackled on and . . .

'Welcome to the 80th Three Coves Gymkhana!' said a posh-sounding voice. Bryony looked across. It was Austin Brook, Georgina's lawyer father. Finn had told her just yesterday that, according to his dad, Mr Brook – as suspected – *was* involved in the lighthouse sale. And that made Bryony dislike him even more than before!

Mr Brook looked very confident as he stood on a raised platform surrounded by his magnificent country estate.

'Could all riders make their way to the games area?' he said. 'We are about to begin.'

'Eeek! See you later, Mum!' Bryony squeaked.

'Good luck!' cried Emma's little brother.

'Ready, Em?' grinned Bryony.

'As I'll ever be,' gulped Emma.

'Right, then,' said Bryony. 'Let's do it!'

*

The morning started with the 'Walk, Trot and Canter' event – the perfect warm-up to get the ponies listening and active.

The children competed in threes, one pony and rider from each riding school. They had to do three laps of the field, and the winner was the pony with the fastest time.

On the first lap, the ponies just had to walk. On the second lap, they had to trot. And on the third lap, they had to canter.

If any of the ponies broke gait, however – going into a trot when they were meant to be walking, or cantering on the trotting lap – the rider would have to circle their pony (wasting valuable time) before they were allowed to continue around the course.

Hari won her heat for Brook Dale, Alice got a second on Princess P, and Tornado was doing really well when a crying baby spooked him and he broke into a trot when he was meant to be walking, so he ended up getting a disappointing third.

Bryony and Emma watched all the heats sitting on their ponies at the side together. They saw some of the older children from their stables do really well, especially Jess on Destiny.

The White Cliff children from Cockledore took losing on the chin, but the Peak Point riders from Nettleton were fiercely competitive, never congratulating anyone but their own riders. This, thought Bryony, was very bad form.

When it was Emma's turn, Bryony and the others wished her good luck, but Emma looked like she'd just seen a ghost as she trotted Piggy over to the start line.

Bryony watched nervously as the race began and the three little ponies were off. Except . . . Bryony groaned. Only *two* ponies were off because Piggy had chosen that very moment to have a (very large) wee!

Emma looked mortified. Bryony saw Georgina

on Beau nearby and she couldn't have looked more delighted.

'Oh, no, poor Emma!' Finn gasped.

'Ewww,' Alice groaned.

'Unlucky,' said Hari. 'But she could still win *if* she focuses!'

Bryony looked down the field. 'Hmmm,' she sighed. The other riders were a way off already.

But they did need to get Piggy moving or Emma would never have the guts to race again.

'Go on, Piggy Sparrow!' Bryony called.

'*Move, Piggy!*' Hari yelled.

'Seaview! Seaview! Seaview!' chanted Finn.

Piggy took his time. But when he'd finished his wee, he began to waddle off down the field. There was no need to worry that *he'd* break into a trot in the walking lap!

Piggy finished the race. In third, of course. But he'd *done* it nevertheless, and Emma had a lovely big Seaview cheer from everyone – except Georgina.

Finally, Bryony was up on Red. Her first ever gymkhana event on him, and hopefully the first of many more!

They had drawn the middle lane, sandwiched between a girl on a black gelding from Peak Point and a boy on a dapple grey from White Cliff. Both of the other ponies looked about thirteen hands, slightly bigger than Red, but that didn't matter. Red's smaller frame would hopefully make him more agile.

As Bryony waited on the start line her heart was hammering in her chest. She wanted Red to do well for *himself* much more than for *her*.

'We can do it, Red.' Her voice was little more than a whisper but Red gave a little ear flick. He was ready.

'On your marks, get set, go!' the starter called and Bryony kicked and told Red to walk on. Almost at once he was away. He'd got a really good start off the line!

He was out in front, but not by much. The black gelding from Peak Point was right on his heels.

'Keep going, Red,' Bryony called. 'But don't trot, keep walking . . . that's the way!'

From the corner of her eye, Bryony could see the Peak Point pony draw neck and neck with Red. This might only be Bryony's first race but already she felt fiercely competitive. And suddenly the Peak Point pony edged out in front!

'A little faster, Red,' Bryony urged him on, and he picked up his pace at once. The White Cliff pony wasn't far behind, but Red was gaining on the black gelding. Then Bryony saw the black gelding break into a trot.

'No, Zorro!' Bryony heard the owner cry and saw them stop and start to circle. Red took the advantage to power past but still managing to keep his walk constant.

'*Good boy, Red,*' said Bryony. And as they ended their first lap Red broke into a trot at exactly the right moment, finishing the second lap in excellent time!

By the time he changed gait to transition into the canter, Bryony knew that if she didn't make any silly mistakes now the race was *theirs*.

She couldn't help hoping Georgina was watching but didn't dare take her eyes off the course to check. It was only a fun starting race, she knew, but it was the first time anyone had seen her compete on Red.

As Red approached the finish line, Bryony felt so nervous she could hardly swallow! But then they were *over* and she punched the air. Red had *done* it. They had won!

'Clever boy!' cried Bryony, throwing her arms around his neck.

'Great win!' said Hari, riding over on Daffodil, the others just behind.

'What a star!' cried Emma.

'Textbook stuff,' said Finn. 'I'm really very impressed!'

'Another ten points in the bag for Seaview!' beamed Alice.

More fun races followed. And now Bryony had got the first one out of the way she felt a bit more relaxed about not winning every time.

She really enjoyed the 'Mug Race' and got every single mug on the poles. 'Stepping Stones' was great fun too, with upturned buckets being the stones that you had to ride to, dismount and then run across without falling off. Hari, who was also an excellent gymnast, had really good balance, so she and Daffodil did very well in this too.

The morning passed in a flash. Bryony knew it would. It always did when she was having such fun. At lunchtime Bryony and the others met Mum for a picnic. Although Mum wasn't a brilliant cook, her picnics were always yummy. Today was no exception, though Bryony could only manage a bite or two as, all of a sudden, she felt quite nervous for the afternoon. It would start with a few more fun events, then the more serious things, like dressage and jumping were scheduled, and Bryony and Red had been training very hard for these.

The afternoon began with the very popular 'Musical Statues'. In this one, riders had to stop their ponies as soon as the music stopped. The last pony to stop was out – and so of course Piggy won this outright as he was always the *first* to stop!

'But, Bry,' whispered Emma after she'd collected their beautiful red 1st place rosette. 'Piggy's *always* first to stop because . . . well, he hardly ever gets *going* in the first place.'

'Don't worry, take the win, Em,' Bryony whispered back. 'Ponies always have their own special skill and maybe being still is Piggy's.'

'Oooo!' Emma gave a delighted nod. 'You might be right!'

Georgina wasn't entered in many of these fun races because she thought they were beneath Beau.

She did turn up for the 'Sack Race' though, which ended with Bryony just being pipped to the post by a ruthlessly determined Georgina who practically dragged Beau over the finish line as she jumped in her sack in front. Red looked ashamed that he'd come second, his ears floppy and his tail limp.

'No, don't be sad, Red!' Bryony hugged him. 'It's not the winning. It's *how* you win that matters. Beau won *despite* Georgina, but us . . . we lost together. See – *we're* a team, and we always will be.'

Chapter 13

The afternoon continued with some more great games!

One of Bryony's favourites was 'Washing Line Day', where you had to race to a pile of clothes, dismount, grab something, get back on your pony, and then ride to a washing line and hang up the item of clothing you had, *while still on your pony.* The winner was the first to get all their clothes drying on the washing line!

Daffodil was very bad at this game. This was because, much to Hari's despair, Daffy kept swiping the clothes *off* the washing line when Hari had just hung them up!

Red, though, didn't mind them being up on the

line, and even when the breeze blew the clothes it didn't spook him too much either. Red had always been scared of wind, but luckily today he seemed too focused to mind.

The 'Race and Dip' games were the last of the light-hearted events. One of these games involved racing to some lovely red apples floating in a barrel of water. When the rider reached them they had to dismount and bob for the apples, trying to get a bite out of one. Although Red was tempted to sneak a bite of apple too, he just about managed to resist. Unlike Piggy, whose head was straight in, water splashing out everywhere.

'Oh, Piggy – *really*?' Sara Wells groaned, as this was one of *her* turns to have Piggy.

'Ooops,' muttered Emma, watching from the side and secretly rather glad to be sharing Piggy today!

'Marshmallow Mountain' was a race and dip game where you got *really* messy. It was the same as for apple-bobbing, where you had to race, jump off, then dip your face into a barrel to get something.

This time pink and white marshmallows were

hidden under icing sugar so they looked like little snow-covered mountains! It was a silly game to play, everyone said, right after the apple-bobbing race, as your face was still a bit damp. This meant the icing sugar really stuck to you so you ended up looking like Santa with a fluffy white beard!

With the light-hearted fun games at an end, Bryony went to have a little wash in one of the portable toilet blocks dotted around the field. She tied Red to a nearby fence, telling him she wouldn't be long. Then she hurried inside, where it smelled strongly of disinfectant.

As Bryony was the only one in there, she had the choice of sinks. She hung up her smart hacking jacket on one of the pegs on the wall, rolled up her sleeves, then gave her face and hands a really good wash.

The dressage event was starting in twenty minutes and she needed to look her best, as marks would be definitely be deducted for fluffy Santa beards!

After she was clean, she unplaited her hair and redid it so it looked neat(ish). Then she popped inside one of the toilet cubicles. It was best to go to the loo now so that she'd be nice and comfortable during the dressage.

She was just finishing up in there when she heard Red outside start to neigh. It was very loud neighing too. He didn't usually make such a racket.

'It's okay, Red!' she called, hurrying out of the cubicle. She quickly washed her hands again, grabbed her jacket from the peg and rushed out.

'What is it, Red?' Bryony asked.

Bryony wondered if he might be thirsty after all that trotting about. She wanted to give him a quick brush down too before the dressage started. Bryony checked her watch. She had fifteen minutes, just enough time to get him to the riders' enclosure and sort him out before their event.

'Come on then, Red,' Bryony said. And, untying him, she took him straight there, where he had a tiny drink. Certainly nothing that merited all that loud neighing!

All three riding schools were sharing this enclosure. Bryony walked Red over to the Seaview lot, found his dandy brush in her carry bag, and then, popping her jacket over his saddle, started to brush him.

Soon his coat was shining beautifully again. But as Bryony was finishing off, she suddenly noticed Georgina standing alongside Beau, who was tied to the fence still looking immaculate.

Georgina's eyes, however, Bryony saw, were not on her beautiful palomino, but on Bryony and Red.

Georgina looked smug. And very pleased with herself. Bryony guessed she thought she'd win the dressage hands down.

Trying her best to ignore her, Bryony popped Red's dandy brush back into her carry bag. A second later Georgina, who had untied Beau, was passing them.

'You need to hurry or you'll miss the event,' said Georgina. 'It starts in three minutes so time is very . . . *tight*.'

Bryony frowned. Why was Georgina even speaking to her? And why fuss over time being so *tight*? There was something odd about the way Georgina had said this word. But Bryony decided Georgina was probably just playing mind games. Although she did need to get going.

Grabbing her jacket, she slung it over her arm.

'Come on, Red,' Bryony said. 'Time to go and show them what we're made of!'

Another flatter field, down the lane from the Fun Games field, would hold the afternoon's more serious events like the relays, dressage and jumping. This would also be where Bryony's friends would do their pony dance later.

Bryony walked Red along to it, trying to stay nice and calm. As they got there, the judges were calling for the first competitor, and Bryony heard them call her and Red. She quickly started to put her jacket on, but . . .

'Hang on a minute,' Bryony puffed, trying to wriggle her arm down the sleeve. Her jacket! What was *wrong* with it? She couldn't get it on. It had shrunk!

No, that was ridiculous. It couldn't have. She must have, she decided, picked up the wrong jacket after grooming Red just now. But no. She'd put her jacket on his saddle, and *that's* the very one she'd picked back up!

Very pink in the face now, Bryony managed to stuff one arm in. Then the other – but what a squeeze!

'Too tight . . .' squeaked Bryony.

'Wait – *tight*!' she glowered. So *that's* why Georgina had emphasised the word 'tight' before. Georgina had known Bryony's jacket would be too tight!

But how *would* Georgina have known that, thought Bryony – unless . . . Georgina had *switched* them! Ah, but when . . . ?

And suddenly it dawned on her. That's why Red had suddenly got all agitated and loud when Bryony had been in the loo. He was trying to warn her that Georgina was sneaking about, clearly up to no good. She must have crept into the portable wash van and switched the jackets *then*. Swapped Bryony's for this two-sizes-too-small one! The Seaview hacking jackets all looked the same: same fabric, same shade, same herringbone pattern. The only difference was the size.

Bryony could feel her cheeks begin to burn as a few spectators started to titter. How ridiculous she must look stuffed into this too-small jacket. Like a crab with two stiff pincer arms that couldn't move. She couldn't even mount Red! So, Georgina's little tricks had clearly started . . .

The judge checked her watch impatiently and Red was stomping his annoyance as he looked across at Georgina. But Bryony saw he was actually looking at something at Georgina's feet. It appeared to be Georgina's carry bag.

Bryony's friends had come along to watch too and were sitting at the side on their ponies. Daffodil, who was beside Georgina on Beau, was also looking down at Georgina's bag. Then, when Hari wasn't looking, Daffy's head bent low towards the bag and she swiped something poking out of the top of it.

'Daffy!' Hari cried. But for once Daffy's pilfering had been for the good, as the thing now hanging out of Daffodil's mouth was a normal-sized hacking jacket! Bryony's eyes met Georgina's and Bryony suddenly knew. The jacket that Daffy had pulled out of Georgina's bag wasn't Georgina's, but *hers.*

Josh, who was standing on Daffy's other side, swiftly took the jacket from Daffy's mouth, and gave her a quick 'thank you!' pat. Then he hurried it over to its rightful owner.

'Thanks,' whispered Bryony.

'Hey!' snapped Georgina, but there was nothing

she could do. Bryony was already wriggling out of the too-small one and Josh was helping her into her own jacket. Georgina's eyes narrowed as she sat on Beau looking daggers.

'When you're *quite* ready,' the dressage judge sniffed, now looking at Bryony too. Bryony quickly mounted Red.

'Sorry,' she replied quickly. 'We're ready now!'

The dressage arena had been cordoned off with poles and tape. On to the tape had been pinned letters of the alphabet. The riders had to perform a series of graceful moves from certain letters to other ones, showing good control of their pony.

As Bryony walked in to begin her test, she knew that the judge would be watching to see how responsive Red was to her. As well as taking Red cleanly from one point to another, she would need to demonstrate smooth transitions as she guided him from a walk into a trot and then a trot into a canter. When they'd reached the correct starting position Bryony stopped Red, waited a few moments to gather her concentration, and then their dressage test began.

Bryony lightly squeezed Red with both her

legs, asking him to step forward, at the same time keeping his reins nice and soft. She then gave a little touch with both legs and they were on their way. It had been a good clean start and Bryony knew it.

While they were walking around, Bryony kept her body relaxed, letting her seat move with Red, her legs keeping light contact with his sides, swinging with him as his body moved from side to side.

Bryony remembered to look ahead to where she wanted to take him, trying as she did to maintain a nice steady pace. She could feel Georgina's eyes boring into her, but Bryony kept herself in the zone. Red was doing really well and she wasn't going to let anyone spoil this moment.

When it was time, Bryony asked Red to go into a trot by giving him a little squeeze with her legs, at the same time softening her reins a little so that she didn't hold him back. Red responded right away, beginning to trot, and as he did so Bryony started to rise up and down with the motion of it, trying to keep her speed the same as Red's so that they looked well balanced and in perfect tune with each other.

Bryony knew instinctively that Red was looking good. He was responding effortlessly to Bryony and had remembered all that she had taught him, each transition smooth and his circular turns nice and slick.

Bryony was pleased that she'd remembered the order of the pathways between the various letters too, and how to do the figure of eight. She'd had diagrams up on her bedroom wall for weeks!

When Red had done one last exquisite turn and come to a good neat stop, Bryony walked him out of the arena past the judge with poise and elegance. The judge's smile seemed most encouraging, but Bryony didn't want to read too much into it, even though she felt that Red had done very well.

As they passed Georgina waiting to enter with Beau, Bryony saw that Georgina couldn't have looked more jealous.

'You have mud on your nose,' Bryony whispered, which in fact was true. Pity Georgina, she thought, hadn't taken the time to check herself in the loo mirrors instead of playing that dirty trick on her!

When all the competitors had had their turn and the results were finally in, Bryony was delighted to have won second place. Georgina was fourth, so just missed out on a rosette. Her dad of course then had words with the judge, as Georgina clearly wasn't happy. But in the end, much to their annoyance, the result stayed the same. So no rosette for Georgina and Beau this time.

The winner of the dressage was Alice on Princess Perla, and Bryony was delighted for her. Alice really deserved it too as Princess's moves, Bryony had thought, were truly impeccable today and her braided mane was a thing of beauty!

After the dressage, things went from strength to strength for Brook Dale as they won a number of the relay events too. There was only tears once when Tabitha Tibberthwaite-Browne's team got a very close second in the 'Flag Race'. Apparently Tabby's team had been 'Flag Race' champions for the past two years, so when they lost today Tabby, who was as almost as competitive as her mum, swiftly lost the plot – grabbing a flag back out of the bucket and slinging it down on the grass, then leaving the field howling and terribly snotty.

All of Bryony's team's practice for the 'Barrel Relay' definitely paid off, as they finally won third place overall. Josh was especially delighted because, after all his training, no one knocked down a single barrel, and their turns were generally tight. They even remembered the correct way to move in order to perfectly execute that very tricky clover-leaf pattern!

The 'Pole Bending' race was by far the most exciting of the relays, the ponies and their riders travelling at breakneck speed as they bent in and out of a series of poles placed at regular intervals down the field.

Bryony's team had aced the heats and as they waited at the start line for the final, Bryony's stomach was turning somersaults. Then the race starter called 'Go!' and they were off. And what a thrilling race it was too! Bryony's team rode fast and accurately, hardly touching any poles. Bryony was last to ride on Red, and as they flew in and out of the poles her heart was in her mouth. By the last flag, even though they'd ridden really well, they were in second behind Peak Point. Bryony knew she had to ride Red like the wind to the end.

'Faster, Red!' she cried, and Red picked up

speed at once, streaking down the field like they were on the beach galloping along the sand. All those days out had strengthened his legs and he was really flying now.

'Yay!' cheered the team, as Red crossed the finish line half a metre ahead of Peak Point. They had actually won, and Georgina's team only got third. Georgina wasn't having a very good day, thought Bryony. After weeks of all that nasty boasting too.

At three thirty, Bryony and her friends went to get ready for their pirate dance in a small tent near the loos. Again, Bryony tied Red to the fence along with the other ponies. It was still sunny, but they'd be in the shade under the hazel trees, which was good.

'Where's the treasure chest, Em?' asked Bryony.

'Oh, some Seaview girls took it,' Emma replied. 'They said they were helping Abi, and would put it out for us.'

'And it had all the treasure in it?' Bryony asked.

'Yes.' Emma nodded. 'I made sure.'

Bryony and the others looked really great in their ripped shirts and trousers, and Emma had modified a fancy dress Jack Sparrow pirate hat so it slotted over her normal riding hat.

They were just adding accessories like eye patches and fake parrots when . . .

'Em,' said Bryony. 'Which girls came and took the treasure chest? Please don't say one of them was Georgina?'

'No, don't worry,' Emma smiled. 'It was . . .' But she stopped and bit her lip.

'It was Sophie, and Lily, and . . .'

'Who?' asked Bryony.

'Camilla.'

Camilla, along with Eloise, George and Max were the little gang Georgina had brought along when she'd taken Bryony's friends' practice field last Thursday afternoon. They were the members of her relay team too.

Bryony instantly felt her tummy lurch. Had Camilla been sent to 'help' by Georgina? she wondered . . .

She was still worrying about this when everyone rode off to the field to start the dance. When they arrived, there were lots of spectators sitting around the sides of the dance arena, tucking into a nice afternoon tea in the sunshine. Lavender had bought a Victoria sponge at the post office shop earlier and Bryony saw the two Miss Ps had now appeared and seemed to be enjoying the cake, if not each other's company!

She glanced from them down the field, and saw the treasure chest was in place.

'Phew!' she muttered under her breath. She'd been worried for nothing. It was fine!

The dance started and it was all going well. The sound system worked, the ponies' timings were great, the circling, the peel-offs, the crossovers were all being done to absolute perfection.

As the music drew to its dramatic end, Piggy was poised in the wings for his huge 'Piggy Sparrow' moment, the treasure glinting in the treasure chest down the field.

All Piggy had to do was gallop on, scattering the other 'Ponies of the Caribbean', then circle round and round the treasure chest, before exiting stage left.

Emma was watching until she saw Bryony give her the nod. Piggy's moment, at last, had come.

Nervously, Emma gently kicked him and

off Piggy went. He knew what to do, they'd practised and practised it, and he seemed to be remembering it too.

'Good boy,' breathed Bryony under her breath, and even Red was snorting softly, egging him on.

It was a triumph! Piggy was hurtling along, his tiny legs going nineteen-to-the-dozen and his long shaggy hair flying out behind him. In that moment Piggy was Jack Sparrow completely.

The other ponies scattered on cue and Piggy Sparrow at last reached the treasure. He circled it. *Yes! Brilliant!* thought Bryony. *A great finale!*

But, all of a sudden, her face fell as Piggy seemed to spot something in the treasure chest that immediately took his interest. He did that funny teeth thing again as he eagerly sniffed the air then his head dived down towards the treasure . . .

'PIGGY!' shrieked Emma. She tried to hold on but, just like in the lighthouse garden, she went flying right over his ears. Emma landed smack-bang on the treasure chest, cheap bits of jewellery flying everywhere!

'No, Piggy!' cried Emma as he buried his muzzle in the treasure, trying to snaffle it up.

Bryony gasped. What was he doing? What was attracting Piggy to the treasure like this?

She rode Red over immediately as the crowd watched on with muffled gasps and the odd titter.

'It's okay, Em!' Bryony whispered, quickly dismounting to take a closer look. The treasure was smeared in something golden. It looked a bit like jam, Bryony thought, except it had little *lumpy* things in it too.

'Nuts!' cried Bryony. She'd recognised what it was as Josh had it on his toast all the time. The treasure was covered in *peanut butter*!

Suddenly Bryony remembered yesterday. Miss Pigeon had seen something gold, sticky and *nutty* in Bryony's tea leaves when she'd read her future!

But how did the peanut butter get there? Bryony narrowed her eyes, now spotting Georgina laughing her head off with *Camilla*. Georgina had put Camilla up to this: to pretend to 'help' with the other girls and then smear the treasure with peanut butter when no one was looking. Georgina, of course, had known full well that snacking was Piggy's downfall!

As they left the field, Emma looked mortified and Piggy was in disgrace (again).

'That's it!' said Bryony, fuming. 'I'm having this out with her!' It wasn't fair that Georgina had picked on Emma and Piggy.

'No, Bry!' cried Emma. 'She wants you to get cross. The best way to get back at her is to beat her in the Chase-me-Charlie.'

Emma nodded. And Bryony nodded back.

'Yes,' said Bryony. 'You're right, Em.' It was time to let her riding do the talking.

'Okay,' said Bryony. She felt her fists clench. 'Bring on the jumping.' She was ready.

*

Bryony looked at the triple bar fence. It was the biggest one yet to jump. Red had cleared both wall jumps confidently as they'd practised this type a lot, and flown over all the lower brightly coloured fences with a real spring in his step – first the yellow, then the green and white striped and finally the sky-blue one, which had tested him a bit but he'd managed it all the same.

But this triple bar fence now facing them looked really high. Red could do it, Bryony knew he had it in him, he'd jumped fences this high before. But he'd also knocked them down. Bryony needed to keep him really focused.

Neither White Cliff nor Peak Point had done anywhere near as well as Seaview in the jumping. Now only Red and Beau were left in the competition. If Red knocked over this triple bar fence and Beau managed to clear it, then Beau would win and Red would have to take second place.

Everyone was watching as Bryony kicked Red's flanks and he started to trot towards the fence. Red's technique was feeling great as Bryony took him into a canter. He was straight, she'd got him into a good stride and was keeping his rhythm even. Now Bryony just had to make sure Red didn't rush the jump or take it flat. As Josh had said after reading more books than he'd ever done in his life, this event was all about patience and precision.

Bryony urged him on confidently, hoping she wouldn't betray a sudden pang of nerves as the fence looming in front of them looked a *whole* lot higher close up! They were just a few strides away when the red and white striped poles made Bryony suddenly think of the lighthouse. Her secret mission flashed through her head and she momentarily lost concentration. Red lifted off the ground but as he flew through the air he wasn't as arched as he needed to be. Bryony held her breath but heard his back hoof clip the post. There was absolutely nothing she could do now. Not a thing!

She landed the jump, praying she didn't hear the dull thud of a pole falling behind her. For a moment time seemed to stand still. But thankfully all stayed silent. Then she heard it. Applause! Red had cleared it!

'Well done!' cried Bryony. But now it was Beau's turn.

Bryony could hardly bear to look as Georgina's stony glare moved from Bryony to the jump and then Beau was cantering towards it. He looked good and strong as his feet left the ground but – wait! thought Bryony – he was flat!

She waited. She watched. Beau was almost over. He was going to clear it! But – hang on! Bryony swallowed hard. One of his legs still looked to be down a *fraction* too low and . . .

Donk!

Beau's back hoof had clipped the pole. For a moment it teetered uncertainly and . . .

'Ooooh!' The crowd gasped and held their breath.

Then down it came, landing in the grass with a thick echoey thud.

'No!' shrieked Georgina. And Bryony gaped.

Red had *done* it. He'd beaten Beau. Red had won!

The crowd were cheering. It rang in Bryony's ears.

'Oh, Red!' gasped Bryony, throwing her arms around his neck. 'You *did* it! My little star!' *No one* would ever call him useless again. Red was the jumping champion.

Chapter 14

'And the winner of the Golden Horseshoe trophy is . . .' Austin Brook paused to build up the tension and Bryony's heart was in her mouth.

She was standing with all the Seaview riders and Josh was there too. White Cliff and Peak Point were in huddled groups to their left and right.

'It was a close-run thing,' Georgina's dad went on, 'but in the end it was . . .'

'Hurry up!' yelled Miss Pigeon and Miss Parsley glared at her.

'Stop interrupting – you bony old goat!' she cried.

'Ladies, ladies!' Austin Brook silenced them with a look. 'As I was saying, the winner of the

80th Three Coves Gymkhana Golden Horseshoe trophy is . . . Seaview!'

There was a sudden tumultuous uproar as the Seaview lot went crazy, whooping and cheering and hugging each other. Bryony was brimming over with happiness as she and her friends celebrated. After one final massive group hug Bryony quietly slipped away to find Red in the enclosure where all the ponies were having a well-earned rest after the busyness of the day.

'We did it, Red!' cried Bryony, giving him a huge hug and looking into his beautiful brown eyes. Red deserved to know the great news too!

Now Bryony felt a desperate need to get on with the other business of the day, finding those lighthouse deeds! She needed to share her secret mission plans with Emma at once. Hopefully Emma would be able to help as she'd been in the Manor lots and knew it well.

Bryony felt a flutter of excitement. Ebony Swann got that too. But the thought of poking around in the attic was also making her feel a little bit nervous.

When Bryony caught up with Emma she was

admiring the string of pony fairy lights draped around the nicest gift stall.

'Aren't they lovely?' asked Emma, but Bryony's mind was on dusty old briefcases instead.

'Em, listen,' said Bryony. 'I've got something really important to tell you now that the gymkhana's done.'

'What?' gasped Emma. Her face clouded over and she looked really worried.

'So yesterday Miss Pigeon remembered something about an old lawyer relative of G—'

But at that moment Georgina swanned past, her father walking beside her.

'Those pony lights are far too expensive for *you* two,' Georgina sniffed.

'Georgie, play nicely,' smirked Austin Brook, clearly amused by his daughter's cheek.

They walked away.

'That was close!' said Bryony.

'What was?' asked Josh, as his and Bryony's friends now came up, still clearly delighted with the win.

'Um,' said Bryony. Should she tell them too? The more people she told, the more that would probably get into trouble if her secret mission went wrong. And yet, she thought, they were the Super Six, who had vowed to never have secrets. She had once made a pact. They all had. And wasn't a pact like *that* exactly for times like *these* . . . ?

'Okay, come with me,' Bryony said. And she ushered them round the side of the stall away from any further prying ears. After one final check around, Bryony quickly relayed the conversation outside the post office yesterday when Miss Pigeon had spilled the beans about Algernon Brook.

'So now,' concluded Bryony, 'I'm going to search the Brooks' attic.'

'You're kidding, Bry?' gasped Josh. 'You'll be grounded for ever if Mum gets wind of this!'

'I *have* to,' said Bryony. 'Finding those deeds is the only way . . .'

She had that look in her eyes. Her friends had seen it before. When Bryony was really serious about something there was no talking her out of it.

'You want Lavender to stay too, right?' Bryony said.

'Sure!' chorused everyone. They really liked her.

'That's that then,' said Bryony, and everybody nodded.

But Bryony knew if she *was* to do this, she'd need to be very careful, so she quickly asked her friends for any advice.

'Go round the back,' Emma replied at once. 'I know a quiet way into the house. And, Bry, I'm definitely coming too if someone will mind Piggy?'

'We'll mind him,' Hari nodded. 'And Red too. And if you're climbing through windows, relax if you can as you'll be much more flexible.' Hari did a lot of climbing at gym and knew her stuff.

'Oh – and,' nodded Alice, her big blue eyes wide, 'be sure to check there are no staff about inside as the Brooks have people who work there. Oh, and don't smash anything either – too noisy, and such a mess!'

'And large country houses,' chipped in Finn, 'sometimes have all sorts of hazards. I read a book on it once. In particular be wary of creaky floorboards, uneven steps and poltergeists hanging round in suits of armour waiting to bombard you with practical jokes that can sometimes get really out of hand.'

'Um . . . *right*,' said Bryony uncertainly. She wasn't entirely sure about *some* of this advice but very pleased that her friends would want to help. After all, a problem shared was a problem halved, or so she'd heard her grandpa often say . . .

Everyone wished them good luck and Bryony and Emma hurried off. It was still busy on the back lawns as people mooched around the beautiful gardens, but already people were starting to leave. The girls didn't have that long before the place would clear and the Brooks would return to the house for the evening.

As Emma led Bryony round to the back window, Bryony made sure they weren't being watched, especially by any of the Brooks.

'There!' whispered Emma, pointing up. The window was ajar, but quite small, so it was going to be a tight squeeze. For a split second Bryony had a little wobble. Sneaking in uninvited was a huge deal.

'Em, is this . . . breaking in?' Bryony whispered.

'It . . . kind of is,' replied Emma. 'But,' she added quickly, 'Mrs Brook does always tell me to drop in whenever I like, so . . .'

'Yes,' Bryony nodded. 'So that's just what you're doing. Dropping in . . . from a window – and whenever you like is, well, now. Did Mrs Brook say you *couldn't* bring a friend when you dropped in?'

Emma thought carefully. 'Nope.'

'Okay!' said Bryony. 'All good then!'

And it wasn't like they planned to damage anything, just get back something that belonged to Lavender. She'd been so kind. It was time Bryony paid her back!

Emma attempted the window first. She was smaller than Bryony but even she found it tight. When at last she was through, she helped jiggle Bryony in while Bryony tried her best to relax as Hari had said – but that was definitely easier said than done right now!

'Okay, where are we?' Bryony whispered, finally dropping down into a tiny dark room.

'In a broom cupboard,' Emma whispered back.

'Where next then?' asked Bryony. 'And don't forget to look out for staff like Alice said. Are there likely to be any around today?'

'I don't *think* so,' said Emma. The Brooks had

various cleaners and a cook that came from time to time. 'I think they all have the day off like my dad because of the gymkhana.'

Emma led the way out of the cupboard and Bryony followed her down a narrow dark passageway which finally brought them out by the kitchen.

'Do you know the way to the attic?' asked Bryony, still whispering even though there was no one about.

Emma nodded. 'We come at Christmas for drinks,' she whispered. 'And Georgina insists every year on giving me and Will a tour of the house.'

'She just can't resist showing off,' said Bryony.

The house was spotless and echoey as it was so vast. Bryony recalled the first time she'd come here last summer with her mum for afternoon tea. The day she'd hoped she'd make a new friend. And the day Georgina had blackmailed her into never having anything more to do with Red . . .

They tiptoed through the kitchen, and out into a corridor. Halfway along it, they passed a table with an expensive-looking vase filled with roses. Bryony was careful not to brush them with her elbow and send the vase tumbling and smashing to bits. Trust Alice to think of the *mess*! thought Bryony.

As they went, they made sure they listened out just in case the Brooks returned home. The gymkhana crowds were probably clearing by now.

The girls passed a suit of armour near the stairs. Bryony got the collywobbles imagining a poltergeist lying in wait inside it clutching an armful of rotten tomatoes to wildly pelt at them. But although she could have sworn the armour creaked, no mischievous spook suddenly sprang out.

They climbed the stairs on tiptoe, watching out for uneven steps. They made it to the top, where a sudden loud *BONG!* made them stop in their tracks, quivering.

But the first *bong* was followed by four more. 'Clock!' gulped Bryony breathlessly, pointing to the grandfather clock back down in the hall, which had just finished striking five. Show jumping was scary, but it was nothing compared to this – Bryony's heart was in her mouth! Emma nodded back, as white as a ghost. 'Phew!'

They carried on along the upstairs corridors.

Down one, they passed a table of family photographs in what looked like solid silver frames. These photographs, Bryony noticed, spanned generations of Brooks, and she couldn't resist stopping for a moment to have a look.

There were stern-looking ladies wearing old-fashioned clothes whose eyes resembled Georgina's: pale and cold. There were men with neat moustaches and starched, high-collared white shirts. Wait! One of whom, Bryony spied, had a pocket watch!

'That's *him* – look, Em,' Bryony hissed. 'Algernon Brook!'

She examined the photo. Algernon looked a bit like Georgina's father. They had the same pointy chin and rather aloof stare. The photo beside Algernon was one of the current family: Georgina's mum, Arabella, in a smart silk suit, sitting on a velvet-covered chaise longue with her husband, and in the middle was Georgina Brook.

There were lots of other photos dotted around of Georgina too. Georgina as a spoiled baby. Georgina as a spoiled toddler. Georgina as a spoiled child. And finally one of Georgina as she was now – spoiled!

They carried on along, turned a corner and

found themselves in front of a narrow flight of stairs with a closed door at the top of them. This, Emma whispered, was the attic door.

They hurried up the steps and Bryony tried the door handle.

'Oh, it's locked!' she groaned.

She thought for a moment. What would Ebony Swann do now? 'Hmmm . . .' said Bryony. Ebony would probably kick the door down. But Bryony knew if *she* attempted that she'd almost certainly get into trouble.

'Have you ever picked a lock, Em?' Bryony asked instead.

'No,' Emma replied flatly.

'Okay.' Bryony looked around. 'Is there another attic door?'

'M-maybe,' said Emma uncertainly. 'I don't really know. Perhaps a small square one in a bedroom ceiling somewhere?'

Bryony sighed. They didn't have time to go on a hunt around.

'What we need is a key,' Bryony said. Less dynamic than a high karate kick but a much more obvious solution.

'Hang on, Bry!' Emma gasped. Bryony had jogged her memory. 'When we walked through the kitchen earlier, we passed the back door, right?'

'Um, yep,' replied Bryony, not sure where this was heading. 'So . . .'

'So, was there a rack of keys there?' asked Emma. 'We keep all our keys by our back door.'

'So do we,' said Bryony. 'But I didn't notice. Maybe?'

Emma told Bryony to stay put and hurried back down to the kitchen to check. A few minutes later she was back – with a huge bunch of keys in her hand.

'Brilliant!' smiled Bryony. 'But we need to work fast. Quick, let's try them in the lock.'

They dived to the door and started testing out the keys. Bryony was aware that time was running out but there were so many keys! The Brooks, she knew, could be back home at any minute.

'We've already tried that one!' Bryony gasped as yet another key refused to turn.

'Have we?'

'Yes! Or . . . have we?' Bryony shook her head. 'I can't remember!'

She was getting desperate and suddenly hated keys – big ones, small ones, thick ones, thin ones, and especially ones that wouldn't turn!

Then suddenly *click!* – a completely boring-looking key actually turned in the lock!

'That's it!' cried Bryony.

'We did it!' gasped Emma. They were in!

The attic was quite gloomy and full of all sorts of things: furniture, ornaments, old suitcases and trunks, heavy folded curtains from another time. But at least everything had been ordered and stacked up neatly.

In one corner was a pile of paperwork near a few old bags and briefcases. Bryony rifled through the briefcases at once but none of them looked like the one Lavender had said she remembered that day the lawyer had visited her father.

'It's meant to look like an old-fashioned doctor's bag, Em,' she said. 'And it's got initials on the front – W A B.'

'Hang on!' said Emma. 'I thought you said the Brooks' old relative was called Algy-something?'

'He was,' replied Bryony, 'Algernon Brook,

but lots of people back then were known by their middle name – I-I think. And *his* middle name was Algernon, I'm guessing, see?'

Emma looked confused. Like she didn't see at all. But it made perfect sense to Bryony.

The girls continued to search but there appeared to be no briefcase like the one they were looking for so they ransacked the pile of letters and papers instead.

'Nope,' said Bryony finally. 'No lighthouse deeds anywhere.'

'That means . . .' said Emma.

'Yeah,' Bryony sighed. 'Lavender can't stay, and we can't save her lighthouse after all.'

All the excitement she'd felt at the gymkhana earlier had now left her entirely.

'I guess we'd better go,' she sighed. But suddenly the attic door gave a creak, then closed with an almighty *SLAM!*

'Hey, what's going on?' Bryony gasped.

Emma shook her head, looking petrified. Then they heard the key turn in the lock, and from the other side of the attic door came a familiar voice . . .

'How *dare* you snoop in *my* house?' called

Georgina. 'Well, enjoy your dark overnight stay – and it serves you right!'

'Georgina! Let us out!' Bryony cried.

'*Please*,' Emma added with a wail. But Georgina Brook's footsteps sounded on the stairs. She'd meant what she said. She was leaving them there all night!

'My dad,' gasped Emma. 'He'll be so worried.'

'She'll be back,' said Bryony. 'She just said she'd leave us here to wind us up, that's all. Don't worry, Em.'

But deep down Bryony wasn't that sure. Georgina Brook, she knew, was capable of anything . . .

*

'I'm so sorry, Em,' Bryony said, what felt like *hours* later. They were still up in Georgina's attic and it was starting to get properly dark now.

Emma shivered. 'It's o-okay,' she said quietly. 'You were only d-doing it for Lavender.'

Bryony sighed, and they sat for a while just quietly thinking to themselves. No Lavender Lighthouse Tearooms, thought Bryony. And even with Josh covering for her, surely her mum would be wondering where she was by now. Red would too! She always, always tucked him up at night.

Bryony checked her watch, squinting through the darkness. It wasn't even six-thirty. It was going to be one long night.

She sat back to see a spider watching them pompously from the middle of his web on one of the low cross-beams. 'Even the *spiders* in this house are stuck up,' Bryony groaned, when . . .

Click!

A key had suddenly turned in the lock. The girls jumped to their feet. '*Georgina!*' hissed Bryony. '*She must have come back after all!*'

The door then opened but it was not Georgina. It was Hari, looking very pleased with herself.

'Hari!' cried Bryony.

'Thanks for coming!' gasped Emma. 'But how did you get inside?'

'Shimmied up the drainpipe, didn't I?' smiled Hari. 'Then slipped in through Miss Muck's bedroom window! And luckily she left the attic key in the lock so really it was a piece of cake!'

As they tiptoed out through the attic door,

Bryony was so nervous she had goosebumps all up her arms. If they were spotted they'd be in big trouble. But even if they managed to get out, what was stopping Georgina just telling on them when she found the attic empty?

Bryony decided she couldn't worry about that now. They just needed to get out of there fast. But then, as they were heading down the main stairs, in her haste Emma tripped on an uneven step and tumbled down the rest of the way.

'Arggh!' she cried, landing at the bottom in a heap.

'Em!' cried the others, rushing after her.

'I'm fine!' Emma whispered. But her fall had caused *such* a racket.

Suddenly they could hear footsteps in the dining room. *Somebody was coming!*

'Quick!' Bryony pulled Emma to her feet. '*Run!*'

They sprinted across the hall and Bryony took a chance that the front door would be unlocked now, and to her relief it was. She pulled it open and they raced outside.

'Quick!' said Emma, now taking the lead. 'Follow me!'

Emma knew a secret short cut to her cottage, called Pheasant Walk. She hurried them into the dark tangled labyrinth, full of brambles and thorns, but it was a place where you could move about unseen.

'This way,' panted Emma, battling them through it. 'And watch out for the monster brambles.'

'This is great,' said Hari. 'Who's scared of a few prickles? Not me!'

They emerged red-faced and rather scratched just a stone's throw away from Emma's cottage so the wild diversion in the end was definitely worth it.

The others were there waiting.

'Where's Red?' asked Bryony. No one had their ponies with them.

'We took him back to Seaview with the others,' said Alice, 'and got him settled for the night. And Em, we took Piggy back to the farm.'

'Thanks,' replied Emma. And Bryony nodded.

'That was kind.'

'And I told Mum you had a few things to do, Bry,' said Josh. 'I think she thought I meant with

Red. She just sent me to find you though, because you've been ages. What happened?'

'Did you find the deeds?' asked Finn.

Bryony shook her head. 'No,' she sighed, 'so the lighthouse is as good as flattened and Lavender . . . well . . . she'll go.'

'Oh no!' groaned Josh, and Alice went over and put her arm around Bryony's shoulder.

'You tried though,' said Alice. 'And did so well today. And so did Red, he was brilliant.'

'Yeah, Alice is right,' Finn agreed and Josh also nodded.

'You've tried everything, Bry,' Hari said. But Bryony shook her head.

Ebony Swann would never give up, she thought. Except that was TV. And this was real life, which was much harder.

Chapter 15

On Monday morning, as Bryony mucked out Red, she couldn't stop thinking about Lavender. Saying goodbye to her last night had been so sad.

Mum had cooked Lavender a special 'goodbye supper' which Lavender had really loved. But goodbyes left Bryony with a deep grey sadness ever since her dad had died.

'Oh, Red,' she said as she swept out his stable. 'At least I still have you.'

'What?' asked Josh, arriving with a wheelbarrow. He'd come to help today too.

'I was just talking to Red,' Bryony replied.

'Oh, okay.'

Bryony thought Josh also looked a bit flat. He

got on really well with Lavender too. Bryony decided she should try and appear less glum, as Josh hadn't *had* to come and keep her company.

'I'm nearly done sweeping the floor,' she smiled. 'And then we can rake ar—'

But Bryony stopped as her broom had just swept up a stray gymkhana pamphlet. It must have fallen out of her carry bag, she thought.

She picked it up. It would be nice to keep to remember Red's triumph. But as she looked at it, she suddenly noticed something else.

'Um, Josh,' said Bryony. 'Come here a sec . . .'

Josh parked the wheelbarrow.

'What?'

'Take a look at this,' Bryony said.

As it had been the gymkhana's 80th anniversary, Abi had included a collage of photos on the back cover of the programme. Some of these were old photos from the past, and some had been taken more recently. They showed former riders and their ponies and the business owners (or wealthy individuals) who had sponsored the gymkhana over the years, mostly by donating gifts of money.

Bryony had been too busy on Saturday to even

notice the photos, and Abi had deliberately made them quite small to fit as many on as she could.

But one of the photos, Bryony had just noticed, was slightly larger than the rest. It was a photo of the very first sponsors of the gymkhana, taken the year the gymkhana began, eighty years ago. And the photo showed Algernon Brook standing beside another man – and *both* of them were wearing gold pocket watches!

'Josh – look here!' Bryony cried. 'There are two of them – two lawyers!'

Josh looked, then read the caption below the photo:

'The First Sponsors of the Three Coves Gymkhana: Algernon Brook and William Arthur Bell of Brook and Bell Associates, Brook Dale.'

Bryony looked closer.

'Oh my goodness!' she gasped. 'And there!'

She tapped the photo. *Both* men also had briefcases on the ground that looked like old-fashioned doctors' bags. Algernon's had the initials A B on the front, but the other man's initials were . . . W A B.

'W A B!' Bryony cried. '*This* man is the lawyer

that went to see Lavender's dad – not Georgina's great-grandfather. I was wrong! I guess I'd *hoped* that Algernon had had a first name beginning with W,' she went on, 'as I was desperate to find the bag. But of course the deeds were never in Algernon's bag because it was *William* that Lavender remembered. If only I'd paid more attention to that W,' said Bryony, 'and not assumed the lawyer must have been known by his middle name! So Algernon and William were partners in the same firm but William Arthur Bell – *he's* the one we want!'

'So that means . . .' began Josh.

'I've been looking for the wrong briefcase,' said Bryony. 'And *if* the right one is still in Brook Dale, um, somewhere – and the deeds are still inside it – Josh, we could still prove the lighthouse is Lavender's!'

Josh didn't look too convinced.

'I know it's a long shot,' Bryony went on. 'But now we know the name of the lawyer and the law firm, we're definitely getting closer. We just need to figure out where the right briefcase might be!'

Just then Red stomped his foot and clattered to the door. 'What's up, Red?' asked Josh. He turned to Bryony. 'Does he normally go on a hack now or what?' Red suddenly looked impatient and skittish.

'I think he's trying to tell me I should get out and look for that briefcase!' cried Bryony.

Josh shrugged. 'Where to then?'

Bryony thought. 'We should go and find Miss Pigeon. See if she can shed any more light on Mr Bell. She's knows everyone, after all. Come on, Red!'

Bryony tacked him up in record time, jumped on and set off at once, Josh following behind them on his bike.

'This mystery stuff does my head in,' called Josh. 'But I'm not gonna lie – it's quite cool too!'

'Only,' called back Bryony, 'if you solve the mystery!'

They headed to town along the prom, Bryony very aware of the time. It was just after half past ten. Lavender would be in her guest house packing to leave. If they wanted to find those deeds they didn't have a minute to lose!

Bryony urged Red on a little faster but slowed again when they needed to cross the road as she knew they had to stay safe. She stopped him until all was clear, then walked him across and on up a narrow cobbled hill lined with houses and a few shops.

'Nearly there!' called Josh, cycling a safe distance behind as Bryony had taught him. They passed The Bear and Porridge Pot – the old coaching inn – then the fishmonger's, then the cheese shop. The smells from these two shops were always strong but today they made Bryony feel a bit sick. Or perhaps, she thought, it was the nervous excitement!

Finally they got to the post office, where Bryony gave a sudden gasp. On the closed door was pinned a handwritten sign:

Shop Shut.
And NO complaining 'cos I'm not 'ere!
I'm always 'ere – come rain or shine.
But now I've gone out to do
something PRIVATE!
(Back when I'm ready.)
Miss E. Pigeon.

That was it. Bryony had no further leads.

'Why today?' cried Josh. 'She has to go out *now*.'

'I *know*,' Bryony groaned. 'Why didn't she know we were COMING?'

They started to head back down the hill, Bryony's sprits flagging with every step Red took. The slow, steady clatter of his hooves normally filled her with a warm, happy feeling, but today it felt like they were heading nowhere.

Then just outside Miss Parsley's tiny pink cottage Red's rhythm changed as something or other suddenly spooked him. He clattered to the side and Bryony reined him in.

'Whoa, boy.'

'What was it?' asked Josh. 'The wind? A seagull? I didn't see one, did you?'

'No,' shrugged Bryony. She looked to the sky in case it was flying off, but as she did she saw something *else* – something she'd never noticed before. High up on the side of Miss Parsley's cottage, under the paint, was a faint raised outline.

Bryony squinted.

'Josh!' she gasped. 'Up there – look!'

'What?' Josh looked up and then he saw it too.

The outline was of a *pocket watch and chain*, and below it the outline of two surnames: Brook & Bell.

'Wait!' cried Bryony, her brain working furiously. 'Could this be where the two lawyers had their offices – all those years ago, when Lavender was a girl?'

'Eh?' Josh gaped.

'Clever Red!' cried Bryony, and Josh looked even more puzzled.

'He led us here!' beamed Bryony.

'Really?' Josh didn't look convinced.

'Totally!'

Bryony dismounted and, leaving Josh holding Red, hurried up the path and knocked at the door. Now she could ask Miss *Parsley* about Mr Bell!

'Maybe, Josh,' she called back as she waited for the door to open, 'Miss Parsley bought this cottage when Mr Bell died but never cleared all his old papers out. Miss Pigeon said Miss Parsley was a hoarder when they argued the other day . . .'

The door didn't open. Bryony knocked again, but there was still no reply.

'Oh no!' cried Bryony. 'Why isn't anyone in today?'

'What now?' asked Josh.

'Um . . .' said Bryony, and jumping onto the bricks lining the garden path (imagining they were a tightrope!), she started walking along them, arms outstretched, pondering things like Ebony Swann would do . . .

'Okay, so say Miss Parsley *did* buy the cottage off William Bell and *didn't* clear out all his old papers, *where* might she have ferreted them away?'

'Well . . .' replied Josh, waiting with Red on the other side of the garden wall, 'I keep junk in my wardrobe, and under my bed, and anywhere really.'

'Hmm, but she's more likely to keep *her* junk in those places,' Bryony answered thoughtfully. 'Where would you keep someone *else's* old stuff though, that's the thing?'

Then suddenly the penny dropped. Bryony jumped down off the bricks. 'The shed!'

Quickly checking that Josh was okay to stay with Red, Bryony raced off to the back yard. Miss Parsley's shed, which was actually a small stone outhouse, had no lock on its door, so, opening it, Bryony edged herself in through all the clutter.

'Phew!' Bryony gazed around. Miss Pigeon

wasn't wrong. There was *so much* to search through, but she got down to it at once. William's briefcase, of course, might not be here, she thought, but this was her last chance to save the lighthouse and fulfil Lavender's dream. She had to give it one final try!

Covered in dust, she'd almost finished searching when, sandwiched between an old gramophone player and a stack of dusty box files . . .

'*Wait!*' cried Bryony. She'd spotted a briefcase. But was it the one?

It looked like it could be the right shape as Bryony carefully wiggled it out. She turned it round and looked at the front. And there it was – a set of gold initials . . . W A B!

'Yes!' hissed Bryony. The case had a lock but it was already open. And then when Bryony looked inside . . .

'Empty!' she said, her shoulders sagging. Then she noticed the box files beside it. They were all labelled alphabetically on their wide spines. She quickly searched down them, scanning the letters carefully until, about halfway down, she stopped at the box file labelled: 'L, M, N'.

Bryony slid it out. 'Moon . . . Moon,' she

repeated, rifling through the documents inside. Bryony remembered Miss Pigeon calling Lavender by her maiden name, which – she assumed – must have been her dad's surname too.

The papers were old and yellowing and the writing upon them was in faded black ink. Then Bryony stopped, her hands trembling. On the top of one of the documents was the heading she'd been searching for:

The Stormy Point Lighthouse
New owner: 12th June, 1944,
Mr Jacob David Moon.

'This is it!' cried Bryony, hurrying out and back to Josh.

'Josh!' She waved the document in the air. 'This is it! Proof that Lavender's dad owned the place and so Lavender owns it now!'

'Amazing!' cried Josh. 'Great work, Bry!' He checked his watch. 'But it's eleven fifteen! We're not going to do it. Lavender's train leaves in fifteen minutes!'

'We can't give up now!' Bryony said. 'Quick!'

She folded the document, tucked it into her jeans pocket and quickly mounted Red. Not only did they have to get to Lavender before she left, but then they had to get back to the lighthouse before the town clock struck midday. A minute after twelve and it would be too late. Georgina's dad – as the lawyer in charge of the sale – would allow the posh hotel chain, Flaxen and Bloomfield, to sign the new deeds he'd drawn up. Then *they* would own the lighthouse and that would be that.

'Red – to the . . .' Before Bryony could say 'train station' Red was already on his way. It was almost, thought Bryony, as if he'd known all along!

Brook Dale was busy, being a Monday. There were lots of extra visitors about too as the handover of the hotel was being filmed by the *Trash into Treasure* programme team who were documenting the 'progress' of the project, and also by the local news. Even now two TV vans were heading along the road near the beach, on their way up to the lighthouse.

'Faster, Red!' Bryony gasped, trying not to think about how she'd feel if she saw the train pulling out of the station. His hooves were clattering on the cobbled streets, and despite the fact he'd just been reshod, the cobbles were slowing him down. As soon as Bryony could, she moved him onto the grassy verge, and thankfully they started to pick up speed.

They rounded the corner into Station Road as Lavender's train was arriving. Bryony flew off Red, flinging Josh his reins to hold as she belted into the station.

'No, no!' said the guard as, red-faced and panting, Bryony tried to run straight through the open ticket barrier onto the platform on the other side.

The train, she could see, had now stopped and people were opening the doors to get on.

'But—' Bryony puffed. 'I need . . . see . . .' She stopped and pointed a shaky hand as she spotted Lavender's pale lilac scarf billowing behind her in the breeze. She was about to step onto the train!

'Lavender!' called Bryony. 'Lavender – wait!'

But Lavender couldn't have heard over the noise of the engine. Her foot, Bryony saw, was already on the train. She was leaving. They were too late.

Then, from behind the little picket fence just to the side of the ticket room, Bryony heard another *desperate* cry . . .

'*Neighhhhhh!*'

*

'Who gave you these?!' snapped Austin Brook as Lavender presented him with the old lighthouse deeds.

The TV crews were all poised to film the handover to the posh hotel chain.

'I did,' said Bryony, nervously stepping forward. Mr Brook's angry eyes were on her now and she was trying to ignore the camera crews on all sides. 'Um, me and my brother found them,' she said.

'Oh, and Red helped too!' Lavender added quickly. 'To finish the job off, as it were.' If it hadn't been for his loud call she would have boarded the train and been long gone by now.

Mr Brook shook his head, his fists tightening around the deeds in his now trembling hands. Bryony could see that, despite trying his best to hide his anger, inside he was fuming, for as soon as he'd set eyes on the papers he had known that these deeds were no fakes. The signature of his own grandfather was there at the bottom, next to Lavender's dad's and just above that of William Arthur Bell, his grandfather's old business partner. These deeds, Bryony knew as well as Mr Brook did, would stop the deal he'd spent months and months setting up!

'I . . .' He stopped. And for the first time ever Mr Brook seemed lost for words but he quickly regained his composure.

'If I *ever* find out you've been snooping in my house again, there will be big trouble!' he said to Bryony.

Bryony felt her face go red but suddenly her mum and Grandpa appeared, edging their way past the TV crews.

'Um, what's going on here?' said Mum.

'It's all right,' Lavender smiled, her eyes sparkling. 'I think – that is – I hope, so very, very much that your children, and one very *clever* pony, might have just given me my dream!'

Lavender watched as Mr Brook checked the deeds one last time, then looking up, he gave a thunderous nod.

'Really?' gasped Lavender. 'So the lighthouse is . . .' She gazed up at it, and shook her head slowly as if unable to quite take it in.

'Yours! All yours!' Bryony cried, and Red let out a huge, happy whinny.

'Gosh,' gasped Lavender, now turning back to Bryony, a smile spreading slowly across her face. 'So the Lavender Lighthouse Tearoom – it's really going to happen? No changing a single thing, mind you. Father's lighthouse is perfect as it is!'

'Maybe just a lick of paint,' grinned Josh.

'And some flowers for the tables,' nodded Bryony.

'Yes!' beamed Lavender. 'But who would have *thought* it?'

'Well – ME, o' course!' called a familiar voice, and Miss Pigeon now appeared with Bryony's friends, who were all on their ponies. The TV crews were heading off, sensing the 'Trash to Treasure' story was over, so Bryony's friends rode up and took their space. As they did so, Bryony felt any traces of nerves disappear.

'So the Super Six did it!' Finn announced.

'And get to ride another day . . .' beamed Hari.

'Go us!' cheered Alice, and Bryony nodded and smiled.

Miss Pigeon now bustled to the front and Bryony could hardly believe her eyes. Cupped tenderly in the old lady's hands was a tiny ginger kitten. Bryony recognised it at once as one of Farmer Jenkins's litter. It was the runt, the one all the other kittens used to pick on!

'So Miss Pigeon,' Emma quickly explained, 'traded a whole hamper of home-made jam for this little one!'

'And he's the colour of *marmalade* if you ask me!' winked Miss Pigeon, handing the tiny mewing bundle to Lavender. ''Appen your lighthouse needs a kitty again – even if it's to be a tearoom, eh?'

'Oh, Eliza, thank you!' Lavender cried. And Bryony quite forgot herself and gave Miss Pigeon a hug! This place, and the people in it were magical, and Bryony never, ever wanted to leave.

'And there'll always be free cakes for the Super Six in my little lighthouse tearoom,' promised Lavender. 'And maybe,' she winked, 'a circular mystery-solving room at the top of the lighthouse too?'

'What?!' gasped the gang, and Red whinnied again, setting all the other ponies off too.

'Even Ebony Swann,' Josh said with a grin, 'doesn't have a room like that!'

'Yay!' Bryony beamed. This was great! The lighthouse light would shine again.

'Bring on the next mystery!' Bryony cried. 'Oh, I wonder what it will be?'

But whatever the adventure, with her great friends – and Red – Bryony felt she could face anything . . .

Acknowledgements

Thank you to my pony-riding friends who I bombarded with questions during the writing of this book, and who answered them all so diligently. Robyn and Tegan, in particular – you have been wonderful and I appreciate it very much, and my niece, Alana – thanks for all the help you gave me.

Thanks too to Barton End Riding Stables in Gloucestershire for not only supplying me with information, but also cajoling me through my first riding lesson when I was inclined to not be brave. And thanks (I think!) to my husband, who videoed this event – even though he'll now have something concrete to embarrass me with for years to come.

And, finally, my love to Howie: the one and only pony I have ever ridden. I am glad that you were "lazy", Howie, because lazy meant gentle, kind and slow. I really love you for that . . .

Pony Factfiles

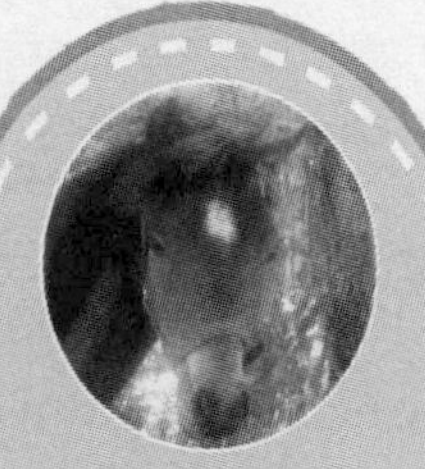

Red

Appearance: Dark bay gelding with white, star-shaped marking between eyes

Age: Four years old

Height: Just under 12 hands

Owner: Bryony

Personality: Loving, loyal, curious and friendly. Very patient and a good judge of character

Special Skill: Jumping

Likes: Loves Bryony, tickles behind the left ear, galloping along the warm sand, carrots from Cabbage Patch Charlie's allotment

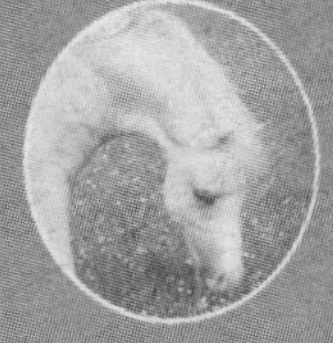

Princess Perla (Princess P)

Appearance: Beautiful pale Palomino mare

Age: Seven years old

Height: 13.8 hands

Owner: Alice

Personality: Brave, feisty and adventurous. Always jumping on in, for better or worse!

Special Skill: Dressage

Likes: Mud and splashing through fast-flowing streams, rocky hilltop climbs, being out in the dark past bedtime

Daffodil (Daffy)

Appearance: Dapple grey Welsh Connemara cross filly

Age: Two years old

Height: 12.8 hands

Owner: Hari

Personality: Has a BIG personality, can be cheeky, and is very friendly

Special Skill: Can make her snorts sound like she's blowing raspberries!

Likes: Banana skins, playing, swiping hats off people's heads, other ponies

Piggy

Appearance: Shetland gelding

Age: Eight years old

Height: 10 hands

Owner: Emma

Personality: Laid-back and very docile. Inclined to sudden bursts of laziness!

Special Skill: Eating (wherever, whenever...)

Likes: Snacking, dozing in the dandelions, watching – but not chasing – butterflies

Tornado (Tor)

Appearance: Black gelding

Age: Almost ten years old

Height: 13.2 hands

Owner: Finn

Personality: Incredibly timid. Despite his ACTION-HERO name, Tor is scared of his own shadow!

Special Skill: Can sniff out trouble in a heartbeat

Likes: Routine, and things being just the same. (P.S. No loud noises either – they send him bolting off faster than a tornado!)

Make a Horseshoe Door Hanger!

YOU WILL NEED:

Tracing paper
Pencil
Piece of card - about 15cm square
Pair of scissors
Hole punch
Piece of ribbon - 25cm long
Stickers and felt pens, for decorating

WHAT TO DO:

1. Place tracing paper on top of the horseshoe template and draw around the shape.
2. Cut out your tracing.
3. Place your traced horseshoe on card, draw around it and cut out.
4. Using a hole punch, make a hole in your cardboard horseshoe at each of the top ends.
5. Thread ribbon or string through these holes and tie each end.
6. Decorate your horseshoe with stickers and draw on patterns.

Hang on your door and enjoy!